Trouble Follows You

Trouble Follows You

a Deadly Press publication

Copyright © 2019 Bonnie Edwards

Printed in the United States of America

All rights reserved.

No part of this publication may be reproduced, stored in a retrieval system, or transmitted, in any form or by any means, electronic, mechanical, photocopying, recording, or otherwise, without the written permission of the author.

* * *

Disclaimer

This is a work of fiction, a product of the author's imagination. Any resemblance or similarity to any actual events or persons, living or dead, is purely coincidental.

* * *

Cover photo courtesy of Shutterstock

Formatting and cover design by Debora Lewis
deboraklewis@yahoo.com

ISBN: 9781672740692

Trouble Follows You

BONNIE EDWARDS

This book is dedicated to Joel and Katrina Edwards, live long and prosper.

thank yous

Thank you to my first reader Jean McGuigan, my beta reader, Loretta Cona and to my editors, Sharon Whitthorne and Pat Beatty. To the best critique group in Tucson, the Savage Writers, a special thanks for the learning and the laughter. Thanks too, to Deb Lewis for her publishing skills and our joyful collaboration to find the perfect cover. A special thanks to Renee Mattas of the Pima County Adult Detention Center for a tour that turned into a great learning experience and to the Arizona Mystery Writers whose guest speakers and comradery offer ongoing inspiration.

one

On my first encounter with John Milton Smith, he wore a German mountaineering hat like a decoration perched boldly above the symmetrical features of his face. The hat sat atop a full and uncontrollable head of hair, the color of which could best, if not appealingly, be described as dirty blond. The hat diminished the size of his rather large ears which were fortunately attached very closely to his head almost as if they had been carefully glued in place at birth and had remained unmoving, yet no doubt growing rapidly, ever since.

I could see yellow, green and blue hues in the wide band which surrounded the hat and I would have liked to have seen it up close. Needless to say, no snake had provided that material. I say this only because he looked like a man who would proudly wear the skin of a snake around his head.

A swimmer's build had him appear quite broad shouldered for a man of such overall small stature. The shape of his face was pleasing. Large blue eyes lit up as ivory teeth showed in a ready but rather self-deprecating smile. That made for an odd rather lopsided grin on a man who appeared from his lecture to be quite ego ridden.

Attending a writer conference out of sheer boredom, I first saw him doing a presentation about his latest novel and his writing practices in general. He was not a particularly articulate gentleman except perhaps on paper. I would have to buy his book to find out. Nor was he a particularly warm man or perhaps it was because the room in which he spoke was cold enough that I had lost most if not all of the feeling in my toes and fingers and caught myself wanting to blow on them to avoid frostbite. It was so cold in the building that I yearned for a release into the parking lot where the sun shone brightly even on this bitterly cold day, and yet something about him held me there to the end of his lecture.

The grin that lit up his face spread his features and narrowed his eyes till they were mere slits in the contours of his face much like side canyons in a wide expanse of mountains. The parallel went further as a couple of jagged bottom teeth resembled the snow-capped tops of mountains glimpsed from afar. And then there was that hat. No wonder mountains came to mind.

His eyebrows raised when he put on that wide grin. What I most remember about him on that day was an explosion of glee which altered his appearance completely and gave him an air of desirability which I could never quite recapture when I saw him repeatedly up-close and personal.

The next time I heard of him, or indeed thought about him, occurred when an article appeared in the local paper which reported he had been arrested as a suspect in the murder of his wife. Having only gone out on my own in the private investigation business days earlier, and, having no paying clientele yet to support myself other than the few referrals I got from Total Investigations, I was eager to develop a source of the green stuff. In short, I had not yet produced enough income to support lunches at McDonalds, much less pay the rent.

Fortunately, I had two more years on my severance pay which is how I liked to refer to my spousal maintenance payments from my former husband. I either referred to him as the SP (severance payer) or sometimes just as my "ex". I believe his name is John and I admit I try not to remember her name, JOYCE. She who had moved in on my seemingly happy spouse and removed him from me as neatly as a dentist extracts a tooth which is to say there was pain and even a little blood.

But I was over all that now and had moved *on*. At least I had moved *out* to an apartment. Having not given birth to, nor acquired in any other fashion, children, I was willing to take just my clothing, makeup and limited costume jewelry. Pots and pans and the like had never interested me, so I bequeathed them to JOYCE. I also bequeathed to her his family, pains in the ass all, and took with me my one and only cousin, Jane, who lives locally.

Not that costume jewelry was all I owned in the way of adornment. John had given me some if not a lot of good jewelry. I had placed it carefully in a safe deposit box to pawn when and if I got into serious money troubles. My change of circumstances had led me to believe that disaster was only a hop, skip and a jump away.

Friends had begun to sort themselves out, most of them becoming his property as he was the one with the money, the pretty young wife and the prestigious address. The few friends that were mine were rather quiet and gave me space to work out my new life, not bothering me with a lot of unnecessary phone calls or invitations. I tried to be grateful for their sensitivity, but I often felt that what I was experiencing were direct attempts to disappear on me and not be caught taking sides. Specifically, my side.

People just usually call me Babe. Or they used to, but in my new life I have chosen to go back to Barbara Black. I'm pretty sure if I ever was a babe those days are behind me now. But still at thirty-five I think I can remake my image anyway I want, short of sex goddess or femme fatale. I hope the fatalities will be created by someone else and I'll be the one to figure them out. And oh yes, very importantly, get paid for doing so.

I'm a Private Investigator in Tucson, Arizona. I even have a license that says so. The requirements are simple. An applicant has to be at least eighteen and a U.S. citizen and have no felony convictions. Not a registered sex offender and not on parole or probation.

No misdemeanor conviction in the last five years (now they're getting sticky) for violent acts, fraud, theft, domestic violence, sexual misconduct or narcotics violation. Now you can see why I haven't even attempted to murder my 'ex', at least not yet.

The finger-printing fee was twenty-two dollars. That alone took care of my discretionary income for the month. To get a license I needed an affiliation with a local agency that has, mind you, an agency Private Investigator's license whereas I would only have a regular girl Friday working-for-someone-else PI license. So, ostensibly, I'm an employee of Total Investigations. That involved a contact of mine from high school who was nice enough to set it up. We were cheerleaders together at Tucson High. (That's a lifetime commitment.)

Part time, I do in person, on the ground, checking out of potential insurance cheaters for Total Investigations to see if people who wear neck braces because they were miserably hurt in an industrial accident or in a shopping mall actually wear the neck braces, use the cane, have the terrible disfiguring limp when no one is looking. And, quite often they do. But I'm looking, and I have seen miraculous recoveries of people who slip out of town for a well-earned rest, poor dears, and then throw away the cane or the brace to go on a cross-country ski trip or a two-day bike ride. Now this would be all and well and good if they were visiting Lourdes and truly had a miraculous recovery. Our local weekenders, however, so often return to Tucson reacquiring the limp, the cane or the brace their injuries remanufactured somehow from the dry desert air.

I have yet to draw an assignment to exotic far-away places unless you consider Eloy or Pinetop to qualify. But I have been successful enough with my point and shoot photography that I've saved Total Investigations clients, the insurance companies, a neat bit of change. Not much of which they've shared with me.

Getting my PI license through Total Investigations was a good place to start, but, recently, I decided to step out a bit, if only semi-legally, and look for some other clients. Very soon the real thing, my individual license, will be in the mail and I'll be all set. At this very moment, hey, I'm just looking around that's all.

I'm, as you know, recently divorced, and hungry. By that I mean literally hungry as my spousal maintenance reluctantly pried from the fingers of my 'ex', and my rather meager takings from Total leave me just short of paying my rent on the first of every month.

More about me. I'm five foot five if I stand on my tiptoes. Soaking wet I weigh one hundred and twenty-eight pounds, so I prefer to be weighed dry thank you.

I'm a blue-eyed strawberry blonde with little skin pigment so I burn to a crisp in the Arizona sun. That's one way to identify me. I'm the one with the dark glasses, big-floppy hat, and long sleeves.

But the hair, that's my most noticeable feature. So, let's get this out of the way, shall we? Strawberry blonde is a rare color, the lightest of redheads, like a diluted copper color on some; on me it's a brown with blonde highlights all with a red tint. That is not to say my hair is pink, well except in certain lights. Sometimes it seems darker. Like it changes with my moods. And people tell me when I'm angry it becomes a bright, bright red. They might be right. But when I'm angry I'm not prone to be checking my hair color in a mirror. So I don't know about that.

But enough about me.

two

I decided to try to acquaint myself with the accused murderer, John Milton Smith, to whom I earlier referred and see if I could be of any help to him. In turn, he made himself available to me after I sent a note through his attorney explaining how we had met earlier, how much I had been impressed by his work of historical fiction and how if he was in a tight spot, and what could be much tighter than being incarcerated for the murder of one's spouse, perhaps I could do some research for him and help him live to see another day.

After all I had wanted to murder my ex and had only failed to do so because of cowardice and a looming conviction that I would be caught. Perhaps John Milton Smith was guilty, but I was looking forward to hearing his story and seeing if there were any areas of follow-up that could perhaps exonerate him or at least bring confusion and doubt upon his guilt. At any rate, I remembered him and looked forward to a re-acquaintance with him even in the confines of a jail cell.

Getting the attorney to set up the visit turned out to be a more complex issue.

I spoke with John Milton's attorney. He informed me that John Milton Smith preferred to be known as J. Milton Smith or even simply Milton Smith. The attorney sounded over the phone as if he were harassed and overly busy with more than one case and that his concern over the fate of Milton Smith was limited. His focus appeared to be elsewhere. He limited our phone call to a few minutes and failed to even ask me why I had called and hung up before I could ask to see his client.

The attorney, Richard Hall, was a very junior partner in a large law firm downtown. A firm that most Tucsonans had probably heard of. The senior partners seemed to catch the notorious and sensational cases that made the headlines of the local and sometimes even the national news. Sure, Tucson is a medium-sized city, but we get our fair share of headline grabbers, the matricides, the home invasions and the occasional mafia related explosion.

This murder was relatively small potatoes. A man murders his wife after years of altercations reported by the neighbors. The marital disharmony was reported only after the fact of the murder, I might add. And then one night a shot is heard and the tires of a car peel away into the crisp night air, the headlights reflecting on an open front door. A woman walking her dog, sees the dark minivan pulling away and approaches the house to find another woman lying there, crumpled into a heap, not bleeding a lot. A single bullet had neatly punctured her right temple and put her out of whatever misery her life had held for her. Whatever happiness and joy she was yet to encounter, as well.

On the whole, I don't approve of domestic violence or the right of one party, no matter how unhappy, to snuff out the life of someone else to whom they once professed undying love. Isn't divorce the only fair way to go? Then kill 'em afterwards when you are less likely to be caught and more likely to feel the relief from your head to your toes of not having to share the planet with that creep.

Well, I digress.

When I found the dog walker, surprise, surprise, out and about walking her dog, I presented, in lieu of press credentials, my doctored cardboard backed and laminated newspaper bill. Not totally convincing, but to people who had never seen press credentials the letterhead alone was hopefully adequate. I didn't have my PI license in hand yet. It was reportedly in the mail, hence the disguise as a member of the fourth estate.

From Mrs. Manning I then gathered the basic facts of the incident, the bare outline of what was supposed to have happened at ten at night on a quiet suburban street in the heart of the Sam Hughes neighborhood in the doorway of one of its less well-kept smallish Craftsman bungalows. The details could have been written on my hand in ink, high school style, they were so limited. Gun fire, immediately thereafter a dark van leaving, a body discovered moments later in the doorway of the house where the van had just abruptly left the drive. Freshly shot. Freshly dead.

And no, Mrs. Manning did not know either the deceased or her husband, had never laid eyes on either one of them to the best of her knowledge.

"Maybe at the grocery store or something, but if I ever saw either one of them, I wasn't aware of who either of them were."

I had to take her word on that unless Milton Smith's account varied from hers. Sally Smith could no longer tell me anything.

three

On the drive home after my brief interview with Lisa Manning, the owner of the curious dog who had apparently tugged on the leash and drawn her to the dead woman's body, I reviewed the facts I had ascertained from a web search.

Like us, the Smiths had no children. Like us, they had been married twelve years. Was it also possible that Mrs. Smith had a rival like JOYCE? You remember JOYCE, the young and dumb wife of my ex, though not so dumb as to have screwed up in the process of stealing him from me. If so, if there were a JOYCE in Smith's life, I would no longer be morally obligated to help defend him and I would applaud if the state of Arizona chose to hang his ass.

I wiped the smirk off my face and shook myself out of those wayward meandering thoughts, wondering only slightly why the person I always pictured hanging from a tree, falling off a bridge or being run over by a train was *always* my ex.

Going mentally back to the task in hand, I remembered the day I had heard Milton speak about his novels, two with a third on the way. He had mentioned his wife and I admit to feeling a wee bit disappointed. Usually when a man mentions that he is married, as well as sporting a gold band on his left hand, it is meant to discourage the hopeful females around him. He had said something about her editing his books. That was all I remembered about her, but he certainly hadn't referred to her as his ball and chain or any other disparaging remark and there had been no hint of domestic discord though I'll admit he wasn't going for laughter that day. There would have been no comedian's plea to 'take my wife, please take my wife' in his presentation.

Once home, I called Milton's young attorney, Richard Hall, for a second time. I assume he's young because of his voice. The high and then low pitch, the move from soprano to bass, sounded to my ear like he had only recently reached puberty. The fact that the receptionist had hesitated before she got him on the phone provided additional information. Her mumbling suggested she was having to look up his extension in a directory and was ill acquainted with both his name and the alphabet and its usage. Not a confidence builder in either the law firm's hiring policy or if one were hoping Milton's attorney might be a vastly important member of the prestigious firm. We know however, about young sexy secretaries, now don't we. How they don't need to be too bright to snare their bosses. JOYCE certainly filled that bill. But I'm not bitter about that, not at all.

This time to I managed to request a visit with the accused. The attorney agreed to speak to Milton Smith arranging a meeting with him at the city jail where he was being held, not exactly incognito, but with little publicity or interest following him there.

The next day found me heading through downtown Tucson and further west to the county jail. I myself was quite well dressed. I had forgone my usual blue jeans and a t-shirt for a more professional look. Today I had on navy blue slacks, a white blouse with a peter pan collar and a light-weight cardigan flung casually over my shoulders. The sweater was also navy blue. So matchy-matchy – so in the spirit of *I am your first-grade teacher.* My usual tennis shoes had been replaced with black loafers.

I stopped first at the attorney's office, or at least his lobby because apparently the lobby was as far into the building as I needed to go to meet with him. There I acquired the get-into-jail-free pass which consisted of a note giving me the approved code to get me into the jail to see my client or more exactly, the man who I hoped would be my first paying customer.

Richard Hall was young, though not quite the fifteen-year-old I had expected, and disheveled, looking like a man who hadn't slept in a week. It could be supposed that when he had last been deep in the arms of Morpheus, he had worn that same wrinkled brown suit as a nightshirt. He was clean shaven which contrasted oddly with the rest of his *look*. Either that or in his adolescence, and masquerading as an attorney, he was still too young to need a shave.

Attorney Hall introduced himself to me. He held out his hand, not for me to shake, but to give me the handwritten pass, nodded and left. So much for verbalization. I tried to picture him in the court room, nodding to the judge and then sitting down and well... just sitting there, hands folded and observing as the evidence and the resulting harsh penalties closed in around his client.

Meeting the young attorney gave me one more reason to offer my help to J. Milton Smith author of historical novels and murder suspect in the death of his wife Sarah Jane, nicknamed Sally. It was possible I'd be the only help he got.

I drove to the county lock-up. City and county share the Pima County Jail. It is properly known as the Pima County Adult Detention Center. The imposing building sits behind a park-like setting of graciously trimmed trees, attractive though utilitarian steel mesh benches and walkways that lead to its massive doors.

The entry area has marble floors with the county logo emblazed upon them. A painted and weirdly uninviting cement block platform where uniformed officers and civilians sit at stations dominated by huge computer screens nearly blocking them from view is at one end of the floor. At some distance behind that utilitarian edifice there are tiered banks of television monitors that are used by relatives of those who have ended up in the jail system. A monitor on the wall presented revolving information screens indicating that the first visit was free but subsequent visits using this system would require a payment made in advance, via the internet and directed to the county. No cash or credit cards would be accepted at the jail itself.

In front of the reception area there is a wall of lockers where items not appropriate to the setting are locked up by visitors who then carry the key with them and return after their television visits to reclaim purses, car keys, what have you in order to go back outside and begin the rest of their day feeling better or worse as their encounter left them.

I handed the letter to the first possible official looking type when the line ahead of me cleared. The deputy checked a computer screen, gave me an Inmate Visitation Form which I then filled out, presented me with a badge to wear and, then, sent me on my way through a metal detector much like the ones you see at the airport.

I buzzed the door open and walked through the sally port which stretched out for half the length of a football field, aware that cameras were filming me as I progressed on my journey. At the end of that corridor I buzzed myself into a large L-shaped room that contained smaller interview rooms each of which held two chairs and a table in between them. The gray Formica tops of the tables were about thirty-two inches wide, an effective distance to keep client and prisoner from any physical interaction.

It was eerily quiet as the doors to the rooms that had occupants were closed. Occasionally I heard the slapping sound of the orange flip-flops the prisoners wore contrasted with the sound of the street shoes and occasionally high heels on the feet of lawyers or other professionals who moved through the area.

There were no odors pleasant or otherwise. The walls were white-washed and clean. It was a stark and institutional setting with a lack of a feeling of threat as much as it also lacked any sense of warmth or comfort. Occasionally I glimpsed an inmate wearing plaid rather than orange and only later learned that those uniforms labeled the wearers as detainees who had difficulty in maintaining non-violent behavior.

I presented my identifying card, wearing the badge that also showed the deputy sitting in the middle of all the booths that I was there on official business. I was assigned a room number. I noticed as I walked down the aisle between the interview rooms to 1267B that the prisoners sat away from the door while the attorneys or other professionals sat near the door. Being sure, I suppose, that if anyone fled the room, the professional would have the easier access to freedom. I located the small room, closed, but windowed, entered it and seated myself. The rooms more exactly resembled cubicles in size and shape, but unlike most cubicle arrangements the walls continued up to the ceiling so that no one overhears the contents of the conversations inside the booths. On either side of the one I occupied the small spaces were currently empty.

I spent a few minutes adjusting to the eerie sense of being here alone, aware that the sergeant at the end of the block could not be seen by me, though apparently through a camera arrangement he could see, but not hear, me. I suppose that is protection of a sort, but it didn't seem so to me.

Soon J. Milton Smith was delivered to my doorway by a uniformed deputy who watched as his orange clad prisoner took the seat opposite me. The deputy then left and went back to whatever duties he had inside the main area of the jail.

J. Milton sat across from me, possessing a somewhat sheepish grin. Could it be that he was embarrassed to be here? The grin vanished quickly when he spoke.

"I remember you," he said. "You sat in my meeting, my book presentation, and you shivered the whole time. I remember that hair and your frozen features. I know it was cold in there, real cold. Frankly, I could see your nipples through your blouse. That's how cold it was. That's what I remember about you."

So much for establishing a professional relationship. He was bordering on the way too personal and risked crossing over into downright rude. I didn't know whether to be flattered or annoyed. It's nice to be remembered for your boobs, but maybe not by a man who might have killed the owner of the pair with whom he'd spent years of his life. Perhaps J. Milton Smith, as well as being a creep, was not the ideal subject with whom to begin my career.

"It was cold," I responded. "It certainly was. But fond remembrances or not of our first meeting, shall we get down to business? I understand we only get about thirty minutes together. Let's not waste them, shall we?"

"Whatever."

"So, for starters, and just for my basic information, did you kill your wife?"

Smith's answer came quickly.

"No. Might have wanted to from time to time, but no!"

"Do you own a gun?"

"No."

"Do you own a dark colored van?"

"Y e s. Yes, I do. It's a dark-green Chrysler minivan, Town and Country. Ten years old. Handy for hauling around books that don't sell. At least not very well. It has an old GPS system that directs me to most places with a fair amount of accuracy where I fail to sell more books. It is not good for picking up babes, not that I tried but I was hoping it might come with the territory. You know the author bit. Look at me I'm a writer; sleep with me, and, no, I don't mean sleep. But it didn't work out that way. Sadly.

"On the other hand, while I was out about my writerly business, my absences, as opposed to making my spouse grow fonder, seem to have allowed her to make lots of new friends and by that I do mean lovers.

"That's what we argued about that night. And I left. And, indeed, could be heard to leave. Peeling away majestically from my driveway in my less than impressive minivan, apparently moments before my wife was shot. The person who found her body, however, insists that the sound of shots fired came *before* the van peeled noisily away. And that is exactly how my goose is cooked!"

"Does this witness have anything against you? I assume we are talking about the person, who while walking his? her? dog heard the shots and then watched you drive away."

"Her, a neighbor I've never met. I don't even know if Sally knew her. I never heard of her. Lisa Manning, that's the name I've been told by my lawyer. I guess it's the right one."

"I interviewed her, actually, I–"

"So how come you asked me if it was a man or a woman who made the report?"

"Just a test of your veracity to see if you are in the habit of telling the truth?"

"My, my, you are the trusting sort. By the way, what are your going to do for me? What do I have to pay you? Other than the possibility of a closer view of your tits, just what do you have to offer?"

"My expertise as a licensed PI. I wouldn't count on that closer viewing of any part of my anatomy. I'm not accepting familiarity as payment in kind. So, thirty dollars an hour and I can document every task that I perform, and the payment can be delayed until you're out of here on bond. I'll bring a contract next time we meet, *if* I decide to take your case. That's how this works."

I didn't have to wait long for a reply.

"I'll need to sell a lot of books. But then there is Sally's life insurance. Probably already listed as one of my many motives. When and if I get that, I'll pay you.

So, looks like you get paid if you can prove someone else did the crime. How's that... and you can keep your tits under wraps."

"I'll write up the contract to that effect. But the risk of never seeing the money raises my fee to forty dollars an hour. And if I were to have to see *you* naked, that's an additional one-hundred and fifty dollars. For my optometrist, to burn out my retinas."

I added a final but important question. "Now, do you know, besides yourself, who has a motive to kill your wife?"

Milton's blue eyes flashed. Then he hid them behind hands which covered his forehead in the classic thinker pose, and slowly answered my question.

"Well, I don't have any names. The guys she slept with, again a euphemism, their spouses or children. People she worked with, people at the grocery store, most of the population of Tucson at one time or another. My wife was not a likeable person, smart yes, amiable no!"

I thought about the sound of the single shot that killed Sarah Jane Smith and asked one more question. "Has that van of yours ever been known to backfire?"

Milton Smith looked up and shook his head, a frown deepening the lines on his face, "Sadly, no."

I got up. At the door I turned and said,

"I'm going to need a list. Surely you know some of the names of the people she liked the least and of the people who genuinely hated her. And I need the name of a confidante. A woman's going to have a least one friend, a sister, an old college roommate, someone with whom she shares her secrets, dreams and ambitions. I'm going to need a retainer too. Let's go easy on you and make it five hundred dollars. Since you don't seem to have anyone on the outside to 'manage' your affairs." I made the quotation marks with both my middle and index fingers. I added, "I'll give you a few days to come up with those two items and also to tell you of my decision whether or not to handle your case."

Milton used a finger to indicate how he felt about my request. Silence seemed the best response. I walked out wishing I could bang the door behind me. As I walked away, I saw that the sheriff's deputy had returned and was headed toward the small room assumedly to escort Milton Smith back to his cell. I couldn't help but wish for just a little prisoner abuse, a black eye, a bloody nose, something small but painful, so that next time perhaps the inmate would be nicer to me.

four

I made my way back to my oven, otherwise known as my ancient Toyota Corolla. Its faded paint failed to blend nicely into the crowded parking lot. Everyone who visits the jail drives better cars than I do. Perhaps, I mused, crime does pay.

I should have been more concerned about my fee. But this was the only case where I had an 'in.' My moto might eventually become 'No Job too Tough, No Fee too High', but right now it was 'Any Job for Any Fee' even if there was not any guarantee that I could collect it. I'd decided I would start anywhere to gain some practical knowledge of the field of investigation just so I might tell a future client that I had experience. J. Milton Smith was my anywhere. Hope he isn't also my Waterloo.

I wondered where to start looking in 'most of Tucson' for the killer of Sally Smith. There was really no place to begin. I tried to remember the contents of the one book I had read to instruct me in the process of being a successful PI. 'Do the next thing, take the next step, interview the next witness'...but without the list, without the name of a best friend and without a retainer or even a verbal commitment from J.

Milton Smith (how dare he give me the finger as a parting shot), I was stuck.

When I returned to my apartment, home and office all tucked into the same limited square footage, I found a message waiting on my phone. The young attorney had called to say that there was check for five-hundred dollars in the mail to me and that he would appreciate a copy of the contract in return as soon as it was prepared and that he would get it to Milton for a signature as soon as he, himself, received it. Good. One dilemma solved.

I got out my book on contracts, found the dummy sheet and began to prepare a document. I mentioned the amount, the hourly rate, and went back to the thirty dollars an hour as *my* gesture of good will. I also included that I would report weekly and that any additional expenses over seventy-five dollars which I encountered would either be mine to pay or would need to be discussed with him in advance. I included in the form a reference to the five-hundred-dollar retainer which would account for the first sixteen hours devoted to the case. I made copies for the file, signed one copy, added a stamp to the envelope to send it by snail mail to the attorney's office. I attached a sticky note asking him to forward to me a copy of the signed contract and the requested list from Milton. Hopefully he could retrieve it at the same time as the contract was signed.

In my computer search I found that Sarah Jane Smith, maiden name Brisconce, was employed as a middle-school social studies teacher in one of the smaller Tucson school districts. I spoke briefly with the school office where Sarah Smith until only very recently had taught, requesting an interview with the principal. I provided information to make school officials aware that I was a party to the legal defense team for J. Milton Smith. I gave the principal's secretary, Clarice Jamison, the name and telephone number of attorney Richard Hall. I ended the call hoping like hell that I was, in fact, a member of the team. Maybe when I received the check, I would feel that I had really been hired. I'd heard 'the check is in the mail' often enough in my life not to be reassured by that statement.

Mailing the contract to the lawyer on my way, I headed out to meet my cousin Jane for dinner. Dinners were the worst time of day for me since my divorce. Not that they had been pleasant when as a non-cook, struggling to develop domestic skills, I had performed badly but often in the kitchen. As the years went by, I perfected a few recipes, orange chicken over rice, and beef stroganoff being two of them that came to mind. Perhaps, they came to mind because they were the only two. I could also make bacon and scramble a mean egg. Mostly John and I ate out and laughed about it. Now its JOYCE who gets the last laugh, may she chuckle in hell. But, really, I *am* doing better with my resentment.

My severance-pay allowed me to eat at some of the finer hamburger joints in town providing they were genuinely fast food places and there was a coupon or a two-for-the-price-of-one offering. Tonight, we were going foreign and exotic and had chosen a Taco Bell.

I splurged on a large diet coke, chose a table and went over my notes on my current, and only, case while waiting for Jane to arrive. She is gainfully employed as a teacher's aide and her budget and mine are very similar. I had only one page of notes. It was with a sense of relief that I returned the yellow legal pad to my purse when I saw Jane approach.

Working with first graders gave Jane a lot to talk about. I enjoyed her anecdotes on some occasions, but tonight my attention was split.

We ordered our quesadillas. Tacos were two-for-a-dollar tonight. We ordered some of those too. We settled in to eat our fill of fast Mexican food.

Between bites I began to tell Jane my news.

"So, Jane, I picked up a case today. A murder case, kinda exciting but also a little daunting and the only witness apparently heard the shot just before my client left the house and moments later my witness found the dead woman on the doorstep of that same house.

"Not looking like he's got innocence written all over him. Either that or she's lying about the timing. I'll have to see what the ME's report looks like if she did call it in right away. Or he's lying and there goes my case. Or there were two different cars that left that night and she saw the second one and thought it was my guy. Can you think of any other possible scenarios where my client could be innocent?"

Jane sat still for a moment. Her brown eyes intent on the tabletop, her brow furrowed in thought.

"No... well... maybe one. Maybe as your client drove away, someone else stepped out of the shadows, rang the bell, and, when the now dead lady answered, shot her and then stepped back into the shadows. That would make the timing tight and if the neighbor, witness, was on the other side of the street and down a way that could make this a possibility, not likely but possible. Don't suppose there are any cameras in the area?"

"No, I don't think so. But I'll check. That's a pretty good idea. Maybe you're wasted as a teacher's helper and I need to think about hiring you away. But first I gotta make some money on this one."

Jane glanced at me. "First graders are a heck of a lot more cheerful to think about than murder and mayhem. I think I'll stick with my chosen profession for a while longer. True, I'm not gonna get rich, but I'm thinking about going back and finishing my degree and getting a teaching certificate. Then I'll be into the big money."

We both got a big laugh out of that.

Jane is only twenty-nine, looks half that age, walks with a limp, left over from a fall off a horse, and is apparently happy as a single. She doesn't date. Doesn't care. She reads a lot of mysteries. Spends her summers or at least a good part of them in Pennsylvania on her parents' farm. She has a car even older than mine. It runs most of the time and her apartment is within walking distance of the school where she works. Emergencies of transportation were not her worry.

I liked her. John had not. She was not enough of a mover and a shaker to impress him. He liked 'important' people, wasn't sure if I was one other than by association with him. He reached the conclusion that she did not appropriately qualify as 'important' either. In that respect I was glad to be shed of John and happy to get better acquainted with my cousin. Fortunately, she had the time for me. We had begun to see one another frequently. As I said, there are not a huge number of social engagements to tie me down these days.

I watched Jane limp out of the door and to her car. She was dressed in a plaid blouse, and neatly pressed black slacks and, even at the end of her workday, looked fresh and ready for anything. I admired that. At the end of the day, I looked more like the end of the day.

Happily, I returned home, had a scoop of ice cream, read the day's paper which I preferred at day's end even though it was a morning paper, and slid into bed in my fresh cotton pajamas. Size eight, thanks to the divorce diet which produces the continuous motivation of "I'll show you; you son of a gun."

I drifted off to sleep, vowing to make tomorrow as much or even more productive than today.

five

In the a. m., I brushed my teeth, using the whitening powder one more time and checking to see that the white of the tooth powder container was still far whiter than my teeth. Another test failed even before eight a.m. I drew a hot soak bath which then took less than ten minutes of my time as I was sure there were important things to do. Just not sure what they were. Then I remembered nine-thirty a.m. was my appointment with the principal.

I ironed a pair of black slacks. Principals' offices still made me feel uneasy in the pit of my stomach. I'd never spent a lot of time in them. But like most obedient students the idea of being called into the principal's office was one that haunted my teen dreams. It also occurred to me that maybe, just maybe, the neatness gene was alive and well in my family and perhaps one more time I could reach for it and see if I could perform in a way that ordinary folk found so easy. At least my neat and tidy cousin did. Just once maybe I could look like I'd made an effort to be on the best-groomed list.

The trip across town was uneventful. Traffic's a mess, but what's new? Tucson still lacked a freeway system that you could take to skip the crosstown trek of traffic; light after traffic light after traffic light. If we didn't have a freeways system by now, the chances of adding one at this late date seemed poor to none. It was the lament of the townspeople. Still everyone continued to play NIMBY to the fullest. Your property can border a freeway, just not mine. Lots of cities have freeways running through the middle; Tucson did not, but the highways and byways were attractive for a desert southwest city. It had been almost fifty years since Speedway was named in *Life Magazine* as the ugliest street in America; surely the statute of limitations had run out on that designation.

Tucson is a good place to relax and 'go with the flow'. Unfortunately, I'm not one of those 'go with the flow' people, so on much of my drive there was cursing from yours truly directed toward the inconsistent and poor driving skills of those around me.

The middle school, when I found it, was adjacent to the high school. Neither had ample parking, but finally I managed to squeeze my ancient conveyance in between two school buses, hoping I wasn't breaking some cardinal rule. I left it to fend for itself. I didn't bother to lock. Most of the cars in the lot were far more desirable to a thief than mine would be.

The office though difficult to find was located beyond a barrage of signs about no guns, no loitering, no... well you name it, don't do it.

I entered through imposing double doors into the official offices of the middle school. There was a bench filled to the brim with students reluctantly awaiting their moment in hell, but, as an adult, it was possible I might get to go first. I approached the counter. Introduced myself to Clarice Jamison with whom I had spoken briefly, but satisfactorily, the day before. I noticed even the grammar of my interior dialogue was improving

"Oh, yes he's in and expecting you, but right now the parent of one of these," and she gestured to the row of stubborn faces, "is in with him. Soon as he expels a few of them, I hope," she muttered, "he'll come get you."

There was a slamming of doors not unlike those I had heard at the county jail the day before and a red-faced woman, wearing what appeared to be pajama bottoms and an ill-fitting bright red top, bolted out of the door of the principal's office and gestured angrily to one of the occupants of the bench. I looked at the row and wondered which child might be her offspring and would have guessed wrongly, as a very small girl with blue eyes blazing grabbed her back-pack and followed the large woman from the room, pausing only long enough to glare at a buzz-cut young man and to offer him her raised middle finger. Young love is apparently not going well in this haven of hormonal explosion.

The principal, a short Hispanic, neatly dressed in blazingly white shirt and a boldly patterned tie, came out of his office and gestured for me to follow him. Reluctantly leaving behind the action which promised to develop immediately as soon as his back was turned, I followed.

"Let me introduce myself, Miss Black. I'm Peter Jimenez, keeper of this zoo. No, really, most mornings aren't like this one. I have seven substitute teachers today, and then as you can see in the seating area, at least seven young people who found they don't like having substitute teachers and are bound and determined to prove that point. Now, what can I do for you?"

"Barbara Black." I stuck out my hand to shake his wondering where the hell I'd stored my business cards in my voluminous purse and afraid to lose the moment by digging aimlessly through its contents.

"I'm working on the legal defense team for Milton Smith. Having no easy place to start asking questions, I thought I would try to find out as much as I could about his wife, Sally. Was that the name she went by here?"

"No, those who were on a first name basis with her called her Sarah. There weren't that many. To most of us she was Mrs. Smith."

"Did she not have a lot of friends among the staff?

"Well, you'd have to talk to them. But the short answer is no. She wasn't particularly well-liked by her peers. Most of that opinion of her came from her seeming dislike of students. It was a shame. Most students like their social studies courses – not really heavy-duty academic stuff, and when well-taught, students get a chance to voice their opinions about matters political, national news, that kind of thing.

"For some reason, Sarah, Mrs. Smith, seemed able to turn what could be a delightful conversational experience into dull hard work. There was, I think, a certain perversity in that approach. Almost as if she didn't want to be liked. Still in all, hardly cause for murder and that is what happened. Right?"

I nodded.

"The thing is, it makes it harder on all of the teachers and staff if kids are mostly unhappy in middle-school, so we go out of our way to make the academics as clear and simple as possible, and keep the students functioning on an upscale note. They have enough problems at home, and being eleven, twelve, thirteen-year-olds isn't a picnic in and of itself. As a matter of fact, I was going to recommend that Mrs. Smith look elsewhere for work. This is my second year here so last year I mainly observed to see what we had going for us and what we did not. She fell into the 'did not' category."

I asked, "Can you point me in the direction of a close buddy? Maybe a tell-all friend she might have had as a colleague. Or conversely, someone who was obviously having a hard time being in the same room with her."

"I think I can find you one of each. Unofficially that is. The friend, who indeed seems to be 'the' friend, it would be a contest with only one participant, would be Ruthie Ginsberg. Not Ruth Bader Ginsberg though it is an *odd coincidence* kind of name."

Nice that he clarified that. Like I would expect to find the famous jurist in these surroundings.

"She is a 'life skills' teacher. We label it Student Success here at Adobe Middle School. It contains some of the information we, in the weird olden days, used to call Home Economics. The curriculum involves skills for success in high school. That area has been added as hands on cooking and sewing stuff was discontinued. Info like how to choose classes, how to study for tests, set up a timetable for studying and other simple information. And some of these kids will be on their own sooner than they might want to be. So, they learn about banking, checking and debit accounts, savings etc."

For a moment in time I thought back fondly of my time in 'home ec' as we called it then. Hadn't thought of myself as a product of weird olden days. No wonder kids disliked their former junior high now middle-school principals. One thing you can count on in education is the ever-evolving ever-changing nomenclature. I began listening again as Jimenez went on, and on. It is a truism that most educators can be quite *wordy*.

"We also show them a little about how to use social media and what to do if they are bullied or intimidated on it. It's a loosie-goosy curriculum but appropriate for this age group. It's an eighth grade, end of middle-school, prep for high-school class. Miss Ginsberg is kind of loosie-goosy herself, but the kids, mostly, like her and the class is pretty much a non-tested, non-graded orientation kind of course. Her planning period is third period. I can arrange for you to see her then, if she wants to. She doesn't have to do so. You are not police, got no rights in that area unless someone wants to talk to you."

Apparently, he didn't think much of my chosen occupation, but his facts were unfortunately correct. No one 'has to' talk to a PI.

"Ruth, Miss Ginsberg, likes the sound of her own voice so she'll probably talk to you. Keeping track of her conversation is a little difficult as she tends to hop from subject to subject without seeming to connect between them. Your job will be simple; it'll be a test of your listening and tracking skills.

"Now for her opposite. This is a wide-open field with rather a lot of contestants. For the winning entry I would choose the person on staff who seemed to dislike Sarah Smith with the greatest intensity. Joseph Carpenter. And he's free right now. If you want, I'll inquire if he will talk to you about Sarah."

Peter Jimenez switched over a toggle on his desk. I noticed it was encased in a little black box with the motto 'just do it' written on the base, the resulting sound came through as shrill and insistent.

"Y e e ssss."

"Joseph, I've got a Ms. Black here in the office who would like to speak with you. She's on the defense team for Milton Smith, who is accused of murdering our very own Sarah Smith. She's trying to figure out as much as she can about the Sarah Smith we knew here at work. Can you help her?"

"First of all, that man needs no defense. Sure, send her down. I've got twenty-five minutes left in my planning period. That ought to be enough time to describe our Sarah... well never mind. I imagine I am on speaker phone, so I'd best be discreet."

Jimenez turned to face me, a smirk tugging at the corners of his mouth. "Room 212, up the stairs which are to the right of the office door and then a right again on the second floor. He'll have students in approximately twenty minutes, so you'll have to limit your interview to that time frame. He'll give you an over-view of Sarah Smith's reputation here, and you'll find it much as I have indicated. Just don't quote us to the newspapers or in court, and you can ask any questions you want."

I rose from my chair, said a quick thank you, and headed for the door. The same crew of suspects were lined up in chairs much as they had been when I entered. There was an empty chair between each student. Obviously in my absence there had been some interaction among the motley crew. The students wore nearly identical scowls on their pimply faces and Clarice Jones gave a curt nod as I let myself out of the office. She had probably not enjoyed the delay my visit had provided. It had left her with even more quality time with the mob.

Fortunately, the hallways were empty. Classes were in session so my chance of being run over by a gaggle of pre-teens was limited. I quickly made my way up the staircase to my right, noticing the peculiar smell of sweat, dirty socks. Axe, though a potent smell, was not strong enough to disguise body odors lingering in the halls.

A quick right-turn at the top of the stairs brought me face to face with the closed door of room 212. I knocked and then entered as I heard the by now familiar 'y e e sss' ushering forth from behind the door.

When I entered, I found a tubby man, almost as wide as he was tall standing behind his desk. He was not an imposing sight. A rumpled plaid shirt rolled up at the sleeves did nothing to enhance his body shape. He wore thick glasses, had nearly perfect brown hair if you liked the Fonzie look, but it was also hair that could use a wash. He wasn't a lot taller than his desk, but if you looked again you would see that it wasn't so much a matter of short, but more of wide that defined him.

He stuck out his hand. I shook it and introduced myself. "I'm Barbara Black." I didn't see a need to elaborate at this point. I gave him a copy of the letter I was carrying to identify myself as a PI employed to aid in the defense of Milton Smith. He gave it a cursory glance and handed it back to me.

He pointed to a chair on wheels that was opposite his desk and sat down himself once I was seated which was rather old-school gentlemanly of him.

Silence reigned until I broke it.

"Principal Jiminez seems to think you can be of assistance to me, telling me something about Sarah Smith at work. I'm looking for general impressions that you might be able to share with me. Nothing specific, really."

"Well, she was specifically a bitch with a capital 'B'. If her husband murdered her, I'd call it justifiable homicide and wonder how he was able to put off killing her for so many years. Probably the man is a saint and he'll be martyred for this. Believe me if ever anyone was deemed worthy of killing, it would be our very own Sarah, the Hun."

Tell me how you really feel, I thought, but didn't say. Didn't want to interrupt his chain of vitriol.

'Students hated her for the most part. She had some unique ways of torturing them. I've over-heard a lot of what I know. She spent the first fifteen minutes of every class period either talking about herself or decrying 'youth of today', her favorite topic. Then if the class period was not long enough to cover her subject she would say, 'You kids wasted time again today. You'd better know this stuff for the test. Use your book. Look it up.'

"She would remind them of their homework schedule as available on-line. Tell them homework was due at the beginning of every class and it was their job to get it in the box on her desk. And most importantly 'with their number on it,' before class began, and then dismiss them. The number-on-the-homework-thing kept her from having to learn their names, an effort she didn't care to make.

"I heard a lot of angry murmuring as the kids made their way down the hall. Her classroom was right next-door to mine, 214. Kids would often ask me, with downcast eyes and slumped shoulders, if they could transfer to my class. We both teach social studies. But they already knew the answer. My classes are full to the brim and hers were half empty. No room at the inn, sorry kids.

"She seemed to prefer the girls to the boys. Boys could do nothing right in her classes. Even straight 'A' students could be in trouble for just being there. One kid got demerits for asking her the date, before class started, so he could put it on his homework, as she demanded. She told him he was unprepared and set him up for a week in detention."

"So not a hit with students. Faculty?"

"She had nicknames for us all. Me she referred to as the bowling ball. Not just behind my back, but to my face. Her idea of a greeting was something like... 'When are you going on a diet, Bowling Ball?' Mourners for dear Sarah in this building are few and far between."

My thought was 'okay I get it,' but I decided that would be an impolite rejoinder.

What came out of my mouth seemed more reasonable, at least at the beginning of my response.

"I do feel I know Ms. Smith better from talking to you and am glad I came. I'm not saying I like her better nor that your information helps me in the defense of Milton Smith though it does increase the likelihood that there are many more possibilities for killers out there than one would usually find. By the way, did you kill her?"

six

Bowling Ball looked a little shocked by my question. Shaking his head vigorously he spoke a resounding, "NO!"

"Can't blame me for asking. It would make my job all the simpler if you had done so."

He stood up now, all five-foot-four-and-a-half inches of him presenting himself to me with a look at the door and back at me which seemed to indicate he wouldn't mind seeing me go.

Reaching into my purse I lucked upon the little case that held my business cards. I retrieved one and placed it on his desk.

"If you think of anything more you'd like to tell me, or any possible candidates for the role you declined, please feel free to call me. Or if you'd just like to chew the fat about Sarah Smith, I'm always free to listen."

He spoke not a word, but laying a finger, his middle finger not surprisingly, aside of his nose... Well the metaphor has to stop there since there was no chimney handy for him to rise up. I sensed smoke might start curling around his ears any moment if I lingered or said even one more word. I rose too, and with as much dignity as I could muster left his presence and his classroom before the first student entered.

I'd asked for someone who didn't like her, and Joseph Carpenter certainly filled that bill. And some of his reasoning seemed authentic to me. Striving to make students have a good school experience would make it painful to watch another teacher work against such an outcome. Most people want their workday to produce positive results else why bother. I thought my day was going well. Might not help me find a killer but I was sure getting to know a lot about Sarah Smith, at least the person she presented at work.

As I trailed back downstairs toward the office, the movement of students between second and third periods began. I hugged the walls, but the kids were polite. No one stamped on my feet, at least not with intent. I remembered Ginsberg's classroom number and decided to look for it on my own rather than run the gauntlet of probably even angrier kids still sitting in the office, or maybe new ones by now. Who knew?

I was beginning to think it might be easier to find an individual who wanted to kill Sarah Smith than to find one that did not. Motives abound inside these walls. Serious enough to shun her, to talk about her viciously behind her back. But to kill? Probably not. At least not by a sane person. But, by definition, are middle-school teachers, on-the-whole, sane? I'm sure they all started out that way but... A question that would produce some debate. The field of those who disdained her appeared to be over-crowded. Now to find someone who saw her good side.

I needed to talk to a friend of hers or the nearest thing I could find to a friend. I also needed a picture of her, for two reasons. I needed one to take to nearby motels to see if a clerk anywhere might have encountered her when and if she chose to 'shack up' nearby with her lovers. (And by the way were they real or just a figment of Milton's imagination?)

But I also needed a picture to see if her exterior was more pleasant than her interior. Just who was I up against? That was my question.

I came out of my rumination as I neared the doorway to the home room of one Ruthie Ginsberg.

Entering, I saw a woman dressed in red slacks, wearing a blouse patterned with blue butterflies on an aqua background and the tiniest black flats I had ever seen. She was a mini something, and less than a fashionista.

Ruthie Ginsberg, professor of all things small and insignificant, life skills I think they called it, was standing on her tiptoes writing on a white board. Carefully capping her marker, she turned toward me.

Must be my day for short people, I thought. What I said was,

"Hello. My name is Barbara Black. I am a Private Investigator looking into the untimely death of Sarah Jane Smith. I was wondering if you could tell me a little about her."

Card case in hand now, I handed her a business card, then dropped the card case back into my purse where a mining expedition equipped with headlamps could easily find it again.

"I assume your principal informed you that I was seeking to talk to a friend of hers?"

"Yes, he did." There was a slight pause before she began to talk. After that no noticeable breath was drawn. Perhaps she could do that thing that jazz musicians, specifically saxophone players can do, called circular breathing, because I swear, she never paused in a period of at least two full minutes, to breathe again.

"Sarah, let me tell you about Sarah. She was tall, well not six foot, but five six at least, and pretty and verbal, oh, yes, she had opinions about everyone and everything, but that's what made her interesting. She was married to Milton you know. He's the one that killed her, but I suppose you know that or you're not really a very good investigator. He probably found out about her affair. After all, if you lived with Milton, you'd have had an affair too. And, no, before you ask, I don't know who she was having an affair with. Not a teacher, that much I do know. And not here in this building even if he was a teacher. The man was a stranger to me. She called him Bob, though the way she said his name made me think she was giving me a pseudonym. She would get all soft and dewy-eyed when she talked about him. How long had it been going on? I'd say about four months. Before that she only talked about school and kids here in this school which is an awful place and she thought the kids were dreadful too, didn't come from good homes, didn't have good manners, didn't know how to listen, or pay attention or do any work. Now that's not totally true, but that's how she saw it. How she told me it was."

Finally, motor-mouth Ruthie Ginsberg stopped for a breath. She was doing a such a good job of interviewing herself, asking and answering her own questions, in retrospect I probably should have just given the horse its reins and let her go on, but I didn't and quickly before she could resume her monologue I got in a question.

"Do you have a picture of her you could share with me? A faculty photo maybe. A yearbook would be nice. And I would return it to you."

Ms. Ginsberg walked over to a gray steel file cabinet. Opened the third drawer down and bent to retrieve a paper-back version of a yearbook. But her monologue had resumed the minute I made my request.

"Well, Sarah and I were friends from the moment she came to work here and that's seven years ago."

She reached on to her desk, grabbed a tissue from a box on the top of an otherwise unencumbered surface, and began dabbing at what appeared to be dry eyes, talking all the while.

"I was undergoing a divorce then from Mr. Ginsberg. I suppose you notice that my name is Ruth Ginsberg, but don't confuse me with that old lady on the Supreme Court, for one thing she is old, like really old, and a liberal and I am neither of those things. Though I suppose we probably weigh the same amount. I mean I understand she still works out every day with free weights or something. Even at a hundred years old which she practically is. At any rate, I became the Supreme Court judge's namesake by marrying Mr. Ginsberg, one other reason why that marriage was a mistake."

Ms. Ginsberg took a hurried breath and then, before I could interrupt with a question, or even an expletive, hurried on.

"Sarah was really good to me. She listened. Told me not all men were beasts like my Mr. Ginsberg, but her husband was just going to bore her to death. Little did she know. When that didn't work, he took a hammer to her or something like that. That's what I hear. Like I said, she was good to me and we became friends and since no one else here was friends with her, and I never could see the 'why' of that reaction to her, we spent a lot of time together. We ate lunch together every day and that is probably why she told me about the affair. But I wish I knew more about it. Except he was very good in bed she said. But she didn't go into details. She sensed that I am not a voyeur and didn't want the specifics. I don't know where they met or what they talked about except they were in love and hadn't quite decided if they were going to alter their lives about it or just keep on carrying on behind their spouses' backs."

Again, she paused for a breath. I couldn't help but wonder if she had no other friends than Sarah Jane Smith as she was pouring out information that one might only tell a close friend. Maybe she needed just such a person in her life and, pre-cousin-Jane, I knew what that felt like.

I had begun to sneak peeks at my watch. Even if I could sneak them into the barrage of her speech, I decided that there were not any more questions I could ask her. My head was already swimming from her info blast.

Quickly, I said,

"Well, this has been delightful and informative." Hoping she missed the sarcasm just barely disguised underlying the word delightful and gathering up the yearbook from her desk, I dropped it into my handbag, already the size of a small suitcase and overflowing with junk.

"Thanks again. I've got another appointment, clear across town. You've got my card now. Give me a call if you can think of anything else about Bob. If she took calls from him on her cell, if she met him after work or on the weekends, if she thought Milton knew or suspected, or knew who it was or was in danger of finding out who it was? Could you ponder those questions for me and if you come up with anything, no matter how vague, could you please call me. This evening would be fine, I'll be in."

All of this I said, as I backed toward the door.

Ruth Ginsberg pointed her small chin at me and was blessedly silent for a moment. Maybe she had only two speeds, stop, or full force gale winds in the channel, kind of speech. But I wanted out of there before my head exploded.

"I will call you," she said. A complete sentence. Intelligible, with a subject verb and object and not even one parenthetical phrase or run on sentence. Boy, had I escaped lightly. The good thing about a telephone call is that I could always step outside with my phone, ring my own doorbell and have an excuse to get off the phone with her. That was my plan for the evening if and when she called.

She picked up a pen from her desk, tore off a piece of paper from a pad on which she scribbled furiously her phone number, and e-mail address, and handed it to me. I backed towards the door and with my hand behind me, grabbed the knob while I still faced her, then quickly spun around and departed. Just before I cleared the door, I heard her add,

"Sarah didn't use a cell phone, at least not here at school. She had a land line at home. I think that was it for her."

Scurrying down the hall, I made a quick decision not to stop in the principal's office even to say thank you. I'd mail him a card. Enough for one day. Enough.

Ginsberg's last bit of info popped back into my mind. No cell phone? What kind of affair can you carry on without a cell phone?

seven

Tuesday morning arrived all too soon. Tossing and turning the night away had produced no new approaches and a bleary-eyed face stared back at me from the bathroom mirror.

"Girl," it said, "you look like hell warmed over." I had to grin at that, fuzzy teeth and all, and wonder how one could warm up hell or in fact would need to. Ah well, I concluded, maybe early morning metaphors are not my thing.

Reviewing, I realized the school where Sarah Jane Smith taught, had not produced any new leads. She wasn't well-liked there, but so what? (She was Sally to her husband, the husband who most probably killed her, so maybe nicknames are not always an indication of real fondness.)

I didn't see a motive except for a lynch mob. The parents of psychologically injured children might have formed a mob to hang her from the nearest tree, but that was not how she met her untimely death, unless of course it was a mob that crept up to her door and shot her. Seemed unlikely. Nah, that probably wasn't it. And I know teachers. If the plan was a cooperative one among them, they'd still be arguing about who got to pull the trigger. So, no, no new suspects. A wasted day, except for the picture and an insight into her character that left me feeling that shooting might have been too good for her.

If you are going to carry on a sleazy affair, Miracle Mile was the place. My ex had gone there with JOYCE. Proves what a class act she is, now doesn't it?

I grabbed the yearbook after a quick shower, teeth brushing, a swipe of lipstick and clean if not coordinated clothes and headed out the door. At a nearby print shop, the clerk, bored apparently by lack of customers, told me he could not print out the pictures I requested from a publication without the approval of the school. My sob story, plan B as it were, then came into play.

"But… but that is a picture of my sister Sarah just before she died, was m… m… murdered in fact," and I let an errant tear run down my face, onto the book, but not onto the picture itself.

I gave him the date of her death, the real one, a little bit of truth never hurts.

"I need a copy for the funeral for our display and one for my brother-in-law, so he'll have it to remember her by. Unless he killed her the bastard," I added, changing my tone of voice to indicate barely hidden hostility. Thank God for high school drama 101; I got my two enlargements.

Miracle Mile was not too far from the school where Sarah Jane Smith worked. It was an area that had a few 'rent-by-the-hour' motels. I drove once more back across town.

Thus, began the adventure of trotting from motel to motel to see if I could nab a witness. I struck oil on my fifth try.

In the old-fashioned neon sign naming the motel only five of the seven letters remained lit. It said _ _ N Y I N N. Pony, Tiny, who knew?

The stucco exterior consisted of walls that were once white. There was broken ceramic tile edging the walkway. The small office, once entered, contained a counter, an armchair whose stained arms brought to mind that a visit by the health department might be in order. A small table with tabloid magazines fighting for space with an overflowing ashtray describes the rest of the furniture in the room. Occupying the chair was a tall young man.

When I found him, the subject of my interrogation was dressed in a wrinkled shirt representative of dubious laundry practices. A pair of stained trousers and dirty gray sneakers completed his ensemble. It occurred to me that when gray sneakers look dirty, we're talking slobsville here.

A severe bout with acne had left him with craters in his face. His teeth were in need of brushing. There was a gray tinge to them as well. All in all, not an impressive sight so early in the day.

More boy than man, he rose sleepily from the chair, squeezed his lanky frame by me, moved at his leisure from the miniscule lobby through a hinged counter and stood facing me. He dropped the divider into place and stared down at me. I'm only five four and a half. A lot of people look down on me.

"Can I help you?" he asked looking around the small room as if the last thing he wanted to do was help me.

"Well, I'm hoping so." I took out a business card, handed it to him and put the picture of Sarah Smith down on the countertop. Helmet hair in place, not a single strand escaping the hair-sprayed do, and an unsmiling, stony-faced image stared out at him in glorious black and white.

A tiny smirk appeared on his face and he shoved the picture back at me.

"Yeah, I seen her here once."

"Really," I asked my eagerness showing, "Who was she with?"

He ignored my question.

"Noticed her 'cause she used to be my teacher. She was by herself. Picked up the key from me to one of the downstairs rooms... on the back side of the building. She chose it by looking at my diagram. It was midday and we weren't busy."

"And with her?"

"She was by herself. She paid cash. If she recognized me, she didn't say nothin. But I knew who she was. Coulda filled in the registration myself. Miss high and mighty middle-school-teacher, Miz Smith."

"Anything else," I asked trying to disguise my disappointment in not being handed the lover's description or better yet identity.

"It was a Saturday, about three weeks ago. If someone was with her, I didn't see him or her. Can't imagine her 'with' anyone male or female who would willingly, you know, wanna play house with that one."

He took a breath and stopped talking. Folded his arms, and just stood there. Seems the conversation was over. He added, "I just seen her, no one else."

I asked his name and a telephone number where I could reach him. In answer, he picked up my card and read it, then set it down again on the counter.

"Well, uh, lady, I might lose my job just for telling you what I already told. We're supposed to be disk... discrete. I don't wanna lose this job. You ain't a cop and I don't have to give you nothin."

I thought about dazzling him with a twenty-dollar bill and then realized I didn't have one. No carrots for the horse, a threat was all I had in my arsenal of bribe or intimidation.

"Okay, I'll make you a deal. You find me the registration card she signed, and I'll record the date and go. But I want to see it. I'm just looking for a name, and a time and date. Then I'll go. If you haven't got that information, you're no use to me as a witness unless you were 'with' her. The cops might want to know that. That you knew her and didn't like her, mighta had a grudge against her."

"God knows, lady, I ain't no pervert! I mighta had some teachers I woulda screwed. But that mean bitch, no way!"

While he plied through some cards in a filing cabinet and came up with one, I grabbed a pen and small notebook from my purse. I waited, holding my breath afraid he would change his mind about showing the card to me, but he handed it over and I wrote down the date, her license plate information and the time she registered. I muttered a thank-you and he said nothing in reply.

Walking out of the no-tell-motel I hoped no one would see me, but I held my head high and plunged on toward my car that had its own back-alley vibe.

It was time, I thought, for another dinner meeting with my friend and, okay, only ally, cousin Jane. I called her from my car, and we settled on Arby's. I had a coupon, our cardinal rule being two for the price of one, when available and we both had a hankering for "horsie sauce" which is, as you may know, the less than classy way to describe their sauce reminiscent of horseradish if you are into mild.

We agreed to meet in forty-five minutes. I went home, grabbed a quick shower, I know, a second one for today, but something about the sleazy motel employee had left me feeling in the need of more extensive cleansing.

eight

This time Jane was there ahead of me. When I recognized Jane's rusty car in the parking lot, I became aware that she'd had to drive. Maybe I'd better choose closer locations to her apartment next time, do all the rush hour drivers a favor, and keep her bucket of bolts off the road.

Again, impeccably dressed after a day with students, whereas I was looking a bit shop worn, she greeted me with a smile. "So, how's it going, Sleuthie?"

I launched into details of the school meetings and the time spent with creepy-crawly motel guy.

"If I ever come to work for you, I want to skip the motel guy. But the Ginsberg woman and Tubby, they look like fun. Where do you go from here?"

"Exactly, my question. What say tomorrow, if I can wrestle the key from the attorney type, you know the thirteen-year-old with the voice change issues, you go with me to look over the scene of the crime and look for any evidence? Evidence that the cops left behind of course, as to the relationship between those two... and any clues as to who Bob might be. All I know about him is that he probably isn't connected to her school, might be a neighbor, might be an engineer, might therefore automatically lack a sense of humor. Oh, and she claimed he was good in bed. That's not a lot and the engineer thingy and the neighbor... don't even know where I picked up those ideas, but it's just a feeling I got. That the guy wasn't necessarily fun."

"You're pretty good at picking up on things. Like figuring out I only have a half-day tomorrow which makes it awkward for me turn down your request to assist you as second ranked crime fighter since I actually am free from 11:30 on. Now let's eat these sandwiches before they get cold."

The rest of our meal consisted of fries and thinly carved roast beast. My question had to be, was it actually beef or a synthetic? I couldn't tell. Seems like it had been years since I tasted a real steak, so I wasn't sure of the source of this rather anemic looking *meat*.

Once at home I called the pre-pubescent attorney at his home. A woman answered his phone, a wife or his mother, I couldn't tell. He agreed that if I came by his office, spell that 'lobby', and met up with him, he would provide me with the key to the house the doorway of which was the scene of the crime. No longer an active crime scene, apparently the cops had taken what they needed. My only hope was that they missed something. Now we'd see if I could live up to my investigator title and find something that hopefully incriminated someone besides my orange clad friend at the county lock-up.

The next morning, I rose and checked on my wardrobe. A shower for me, and since my apartment did not provide me with the luxury of a washer and dryer, a load of clothing into the washing machine downstairs. I deposited my clothes in the one available washer, added the detergent, issued a little prayer that my clothes would remain mine at least through the rinse cycle and, hoping the weird-neighbor-bra-thief was not lurking around, I went back upstairs to review my case notes.

There weren't many. The interview of the woman walking her dog. The interviews at the school, three of them consisted of the pro-Sally, anti-Sally and finally, the principal. He was also closer aligned with the anti-Sally column. Then there was the pimply desk clerk at the motel which I would rate in the no-tell-motel category, but he had told what little he knew. For the most part I had to put this kid into the anti-Sally camp. The interview, such as it was, of my client would also go in the anti-Sally column. Well, maybe I needed to find Sally's mother or sister... if one of them existed. Maybe they would prove to be listed among those who liked her. Hard to find balance here and I believe in balance. None of us is universally loved even if we think we are. Few of us are universally hated, though Sally seemed to have come close. Her lover, now if I could find him, that might be positive input. But if I could find him, I would probably be on the way to solving this case.

Time to throw my clothes in the dryer. I had counted my bras. Seven... every last one! As I walked down two flights of steps, I had to hope that the local bra thief had some compassion and would not send me into the world in an awkward fashion for a woman of my years. Melons they were not, but at least they should face forward and not drift in an unseemly fashion to either the left or right, or, heaven above, each point in a different direction.

I remembered why I'd chosen these apartments. First and foremost, because I could afford them. Located near Craycroft and the Air Force base, Davis Monthan, they were near my bank. Convenient, if and when I ever had a check to deposit. They were in a rather safe environment. Covered parking and utilities included. Hell, they were perfect.

My apartment building was small and unimposing, pink stucco and peeling a bit, over-grown and with a somewhat weedy entry garden and a pool I wouldn't wash my pet dog in. However, if I had a pet frog, he might like the near green waters of the desert oasis fenced in with a chain-link which had little appeal visually and produced more the sense of a desert cage than of a desert oasis.

I was in luck today, I could account for all my clothes, though some lovely fellow tenant had piled them unceremoniously on top of the dryer in order to use the washer for him or herself.

I rescued the bras, yes, all seven, and then chose to take them back upstairs to dry in a safe environment, put the rest of the laundry into the dryer, pushed several buttons and was on my way back upstairs.

I passed the door of creepy neighbor, or at least the one the rest of the tenants seemed to think was responsible for the disappearance of lady's lingerie.

As I did so, he emerged. His eyes glittered as he observed the contents of my arms. I didn't know if he wanted them, or if he just admired the cache that I had found and wished he'd gotten there first. There was one other possibility. He might not be the bra-stealer himself, but might spend the rest of his day circulating the rumor that I was the one. After all, he'd caught me bra-clutchingly red-handed.

Back upstairs, I entered my handwritten notes into my laptop. Nothing much there. I still liked the idea of everyone who disliked her conspiring to kill her. But then surely the body would have been riddled with bullets or stabbed many times a la Agatha Christie.

One more trip down the stairs to grab garments out of the dryer before anyone else did so. Creepy neighbor's door was once again closed and this time it remained so. The walls in the stairwell were marred as if someone had climbed them, kicking muddy shoes against dingy gray walls on every third step. Upstairs again, I began the arduous chore of folding, hanging and putting away. Why isn't there a machine for that and if there were, could I afford it? Think *it's* called a *maid,* and the answer is no! I could not!

nine

I had arranged to pick Jane up at her school and take her to lunch, my treat so it would have to be someplace cheap, and then go on to the home formerly occupied by Sally, deceased, and her ever-lovin' husband, Milton, incarcerated. No need to worry about either of them coming by to see what we were up to. Going downtown to the young attorney's lobby and retrieving the key was to be my first action of the day related to solving the murder.

Parking was always an issue downtown, so I had to walk several blocks to experience the same wordless exchange as I had encountered earlier. Maybe the boy lawyer couldn't talk. Well, no, on the phone he had shown me, though truly in very few words, that at least he possessed the power of speech.

I left our 'lobby' encounter and made my way back to my car dodging traffic as I crossed the street in the middle of the block. If the attorney had an actual office, apparently, I was never to see it. I began to ruminate about our brief meetings. He was very young! It had to be his mother I had spoken with on the phone. She called him "Richie" when she directed him to take the call. It definitely had that fifties ring to it, not at all the voice of one who had just enjoyed morning sex. Yeah, most likely mother, not wife or lover

I let my mind play with fantasies. In the lobby, he had handed me a plain white envelope. I could feel the key shape inside when I grasped it. But what if it were say the wafer from the very first communion of the Catholic church, like year one, very first. And we were being stalked by a mob of anti-Catholics. Or what if it were indeed the key to a treasure chest that lay immersed under tons of water in the Indian Ocean, and the map were in the mail. It could have been so many mysterious and important and secret things. Not just the key to a small bungalow, Craftsman style, in the heart of the Sam Hughes neighborhood where a highly unpopular lady had met a swift and sudden end. But, unfortunately, that is exactly what it was. No high drama here unless I found some waiting at the other end of the drive.

I picked up Jane, my fellow junior detective, in the driveway of her school. It was fun to see the teachers in cut-offs and t-shirts enjoying a rare day without students or parents to monitor their every move.

"What was the all-important message of today's seminar?"

Jane slammed the car door. "Safety from Sexual Predators." I myself haven't seen any around. I could use a sexual predator or two in my life right now, but, apparently, they haven't any to spare that are interested in middle-aged school teacher types. Well, at least it was more interesting than the usual fare,

'Sensational bulletin boards and how to make them.' That kinda thing is par for the course in these sessions when we are already champing at the bit to get out of the library and spruce up our rooms. So, did you get the key?"

"Yep, right out of the hands of Talkative Tommy or as his mommy calls him 'Richie'. By the by, how do you get off labeling yourself as middle-aged? Since when is twenty-nine middle-aged?"

Jane said, "Well, you probably hadn't noticed but I have been twenty-nine on my last three birthdays. Not an attractive habit, lying about one's age, but then since you never picked up on it, perhaps I'm a successful prevaricator."

"Still," I said, "that only makes you thirty-one. I, myself am thirty-five, and that's definitely not middle-aged, unless you're not planning on making it to seventy?"

"Your addition is somewhat questionable, but over-looking your math deficiencies, I'm young then, by your definition, and hungry. Feed me. Where today, oh queen of coupons?"

"Out of coupons for a change. Let's go wild and chow down at one of those Big Bear or Brown Bear or something like that restaurants. I understand the food's not that great but at least it comes in huge portions."

"I'm on for that," Jane said. She never over-indulged, was a lithe one hundred and ten pounds, and always crisply dressed. Her short, shiny brown hair accented a face with regular features and a warm, even smile. Her limp, acquired in a short woman's fall from an exceedingly tall horse, was her only limiting handicap. And yet the men did not flock around her. Single attractive young women should never work in elementary schools. Employment in that level of education usually ends up being the no-men-land for even pleasant looking virgins.

After a quick lunch, we got into my car and drove to the Sam Hughes neighborhood and the home of Sally and Milton Smith. Looking small and unkempt, the wire cut brick with sallow brown trim appeared at the end of a short driveway. The attached carport enclosed an older Chevy Impala leaving no room on either side of the auto for the most careful of drivers to make even a slight error. Blue, undented and in need of a wash, the car was enclosed in a carport which itself was surrounded by large rose bushes on either side. Since it had only the capacity for one car, that implied tandem parking. I could imagine the arguments over trying to decide which of them would leave the house first thing in the morning.

I realized that in an embarrassing oversight I had failed to ascertain what Milton did for a living. Maybe he didn't leave in the morning. Maybe he stayed home and wrote books that didn't sell very well. I wondered if he did something more lucrative to fill the family coffers.

Grass growing willy-nilly in the graveled front yard showed the house to be in a help-needed state of neglect. There were spacers, large pieces of flagstone, that produced a somewhat uneven path toward the front door.

Leaving my car behind hers, its hood almost under the shade of the carport, I noticed a door into the house, but the lock failed to respond to the key when I probed its interior workings. We made our way to the front door walking by a box hedge that sat droopily in the bright sunlight. I wondered if it was an appropriate use of a private detective's time to stop to water and weed. The grounds could certainly use some care. The yellow crime tape was no longer pulled tightly across the door, but rather dangled like a formerly festive, now forlorn, banner. Depression seemed to follow us inside.

Deposited through the letter flap a small and disorderly pile of mail and sales flyers had accumulated. They seemed to move toward us as we walked through the front door. It was the kind of Stephen King scene that made me wish I was armed and dangerous and could draw my handgun and proceed to check out the scene for miscreants. Alas I had no gun.

I motioned for Jane to stay behind as I walked from the living room down a short hallway and opened doors to inspect two small rooms, a study and a guest bedroom. At the end of the hall, I found a rather large master bedroom suite. Much to my relief, these rooms appeared to lack human or animal occupants. The plain bedroom suite with its simple bed coverings and stern oak finishes relieved my anxiety. No living thing occupied the space and it was too uninviting to be haunted. Even ghosts like a little welcoming ambience.

Back in the living room, I found Jane ensconced on an uncomfortable looking Danish modern sofa, reading a copy of *Arizona Mansions* she appeared to have found in a stack of similar sized magazines on the coffee table, teak, with modern lines and unlovely curves, the table not Jane.

Leaving the living room through an arched doorway, I walked into a kitchen. This room large in comparison to the other rooms in the rest of the house included a small dining table at one end as well as appliances and a princely amount of cabinets and countertops unadorned by so much as a cookie jar, or a cache of cooking utensils. Off that room was a service porch with a washer and dryer, matching white and ordinary, standing empty in the small space between the open kitchen door and the door to the back yard.

Returning to the kitchen, I opened the refrigerator in the hope that it might not contain a bunch of spoiled food. And there, as luck would have it, was an almost barren interior. Could it be that some kind soul, family member or friend, had come and removed spoilable objects or was this a family whose frig only contained jelly, margarine and condiment packages from fast food chains? Had I found one more sign that this family home might not have been a household of contentment and domestic bliss? It was as personal as a hotel suite without the pleasing décor.

Back in the living room, I observed that there was a door at the far end that was closed with a dead-bolt lock. Assumedly it led into the carport. And that was that. One bathroom, three bedrooms, kitchen, utility room, and a large sparsely furnished living room seemed to describe the footprint of the house. Whatever Milton and Sally could be said to be proud of, it was certainly not their DIY decorating skills.

ten

"How about we start on the study?"

Jane reluctantly cast aside her copy of *Arizona Mansions*. "And just as I was about to pick out the appropriate home for me to live in."

She followed me down the hall to a room which held, if somewhat awkwardly, two of everything, desks, chairs, lamps and the obvious space where two laptop computers had, in the recent past, rested as indicated by the size of the dust free rectangles on the otherwise dust ridden surfaces. Plugs remained, printers, again matching, remained, but the laptops had apparently been seized. I had to hope that my client had not had lots of incriminating web sites or web searches for that matter on his computer. Awkward things like "How to Murder your Spouse and Not Be Caught".

On the other hand, perhaps Sally Smith had found a link to "Cheating and How to Get Away with It." Or perhaps just matchmaking sights which might or might not be helpful in finding the illusive lover. It was of course, questionable as to whether or not local law enforcement would follow up on such leads. Did they need to find the lover, since they had so handily settled on my J. Milton Smith as the dude who did the lady in?

Lacking computers, and perhaps the skills to search them, if we had indeed had the opportunity, I opted for the file cabinet stuck in dull greyness in a corner of the room. Jane began her search through desk drawers.

It became abundantly clear that Milton was the organized one. Apparently, his wife kept any and all artifacts that might, or more likely might not, be needed at some future point in time. Surely irritating to a neat freak but not necessarily a motive for murder. And definitely a common dilemma of many a schoolteacher who often thought "I can use these for the unit on..."

I heard a "tsk, tsk" as Jane began to empty out the contents of the center drawer which among other things held a disarray of business cards and not a few empty candy wrappers, a cork, various and sundry scribbled notes on the top pages of small note pads in a hue of bright colors and pencils, pens and scissors scattered throughout looking more than anything like a badly thrown game of pick-up-sticks. I collected the business cards to peruse at a later date.

"What a messy woman," Jane said, her lips turning downward into a judgmental curve.

"Really. Makes me think if she had any memorabilia from her affair it would be here in plain sight. Obviously, no one would search very long, at least no curious husband, who knew her well, would look in her junk heap of a desk for anything of great importance."

There were six more drawers, three to a side, and Jane began to rummage through them.

I returned my attention to the top drawer of the filing cabinet. Obviously a more organized approach had been taken here. The contents were sparse. And not, I noted, in alphabetical order. The first file was teaching certificates. The second one was letters of recommendation. The third held medical records for the current year. Then there was a file for organizations which at a cursory glimpse showed only the local chapter of the NEA. I found one more labeled tax returns, the thickest of them all. One more folder marked miscellaneous was empty.

That struck me as odd. If the keeper of the desk was the same person who kept the top file cabinet then not only did we go from messy to neat as a pin but also someone who is disorganized would have a large, miscellaneous, file later, file. I had to wonder if someone, the police maybe, had removed the contents of such a file. Or Milton Smith, was he the culprit?

I double-checked to be sure this file cabinet contained the records of Sally Smith and sure enough the name of Sarah Jane Smith was on the teacher's certificate. The doctor's office receipts reflected her name as well. Nothing much in the doctor's office receipts. The visit to a gynecologist must have also included a prescription for birth control pills. There was a copy of a hefty check to a local drug store issued on the same day as the appointment and the notation read 'bcpills'. (Hmmm.) Apparently, no one around here wanted a baby. But was there also someone out there who didn't like the idea of an unexpected pregnancy as well?

The second drawer seemed to contain the property of Milton Smith. There was a folder marked "Book Submissions." One labeled "Self-publishing," as well as duplicates of some of the categories found in Mrs. Smith's drawer. Files relating to book or short story titles though crammed in the back of the drawer, were somewhat neat and in alphabetical order. There was also a file which was unceremoniously labeled pay stubs. The answer to Milton's employment was now within my easy grasp. As well as his writing, apparently the other source of income for J. Milton Smith was a part time job at a local hard-ware store.

The third drawer held yearbooks from Sarah Jane Smith's school similar to the one I had gotten from Ruth Ginsberg when I visited the middle school where both she and Sarah Jane Smith taught. And drawer four, the final one, held copy paper for the printers on the stands left of both desks. Not much of a find.

Idly, I began to thumb through the stack of yearbooks. In a manila envelope stuck between the top two yearbooks, I struck pay dirt.

There was a photo, only one, of Sarah Jane Smith and a tall and quite handsome middle-aged-man. Their arms were entwined in what appeared to be a lover's grasp. Probably this was not a distant cousin or even a brother unless we were looking for evidence of incest.

They were smiling into one another's eyes. If Mrs. Smith were five foot six or even five foot seven, then this guy must be somewhere near six feet tall. I turned the photo over hoping for names on the back or a date, but nothing. The weird thing was, there did not seem to be any indication that this was a selfie, as a matter of fact all arms and hands were accounted for in the photo, so who did the couple get to take the pic. Clandestine affairs were usually not celebrated by asking for photos to be taken, but then again... perhaps on a trip out of town to a resort or something like that.

In the background there was a beach and water... not a Tucson view. But no other distinguishing items showed in the photo. Nothing lovely like a life ring with an imprint of the TAHOE QUEEN or some helpful clue like that.

I called Jane away from her exploration of the desk to show her my find.

"This makes the search, otherwise a complete bore, worthwhile." She also turned the picture over, making me not feel quite so silly for having hoped for identifying information on the back.

"One thing's for sure. I have to get in to see J. Milton Smith to see if he can identify this man. And, too, no avoiding it, go back to see Ruth Ginsberg and the 'Bowling Ball' and risk being trampled on by pre-teens for a second time. If J. Milton can't recognize the man in the picture, maybe the photo will click with one of those two."

Busily shaking out the remainder of the yearbooks, hoping another clue might fall out, I said. "There still remains the 'his' desk of the 'his' and 'her' combination. I'll go through that."

Milton Smith's desk was as orderly as his portion of the file cabinet and just as dull at least to a PI. Nothing out of place. Idle curiosity made me glance at his tax returns for the previous year. Interestingly the couple while married filed separate tax returns, and glancing back a few years, I saw that this was their pattern. Were they not really married or married in name only? Not a lot of sharing between the two of them. Another curiosity. But still something I should research. Once again, a certain formality in their marriage and a lack of warmth or interdependence seemed to surface here. Certainly, the sparseness of décor, the lack of a sense of home, of welcome in the cold and sparse furnishings, in the empty refrigerator implied to me a death of affection might have taken place long before the actual death of one-half of the couple. Something more to ponder.

I gathered up Jane, the photo, the stack of business cards, and left the house. Keeping the key for future closer look, we left, carefully locking up behind us.

As I drove Jane home, we were both pretty quiet.

"So, what's your next step?" Jane asked.

"Can't think of a damn thing. I'll need to show the pic to J. Milton. At the jail. I guess. And, then, depending on his response, maybe the Ginsberg woman or even other teachers at the school. I dunno."

We fell back into silence. A comfortable silence. That was one of the things I loved about my cousin Jane. Talking or not there was never any tension between us. She had become my best and almost my only friend since my divorce and she was always there for me. Quiet, helpful and willing to spend her free time hanging with me no matter what we actually did with that time. When we got to her house, Jane said. "Okay, keep me posted. Maybe J. Milton will recognize this guy and we'll be able to begin to see who else might have done in dear old Sal!"

Jane opened the door, literally hopped out and waved in the process of closing her door and was gone.

On the way to my apartment, I tried to let my imagination take over. What could possibly be the intricacies of working this out? I was drawing a big blank.

Nothing to see here! Something to ignore here! Those were the thoughts that rose immediately to mind. In my thinking about the tall guy and who he might be, I pondered if it was possible that someone or indeed anyone other than the two of them knew who Sally's lover was? I surely hoped someone knew. Having the photo helped me to think I might find out to whom Sally had given her heart, if she had one (there had been some speculation about that), and shared her body with, in the last months of her life.

There seemed to be nothing for it but for me to visit jail house rock and see my client one more time. Show him the picture. Ask him if he knew who the guy was. If he could help in any manner to assist me in tracing down the lover.

Questions. Was the guy in the picture the spurned lover about to be replaced by a newer model? That might make him pissed at Sally. Was he the current lover? Was someone, wife, girlfriend, mother, upset by his liaison with Sally Smith? Was there a past lover or only a current one?

Did J. Milton Smith know him or know about him? Would that have been enough to drive my client to kill his wife? Not from what I saw of their lives together. You've got to love with passion to kill the disrupter of your marriage. I might have done in JOYCE. Surely, she had it coming. But I felt strongly, passionately about JOYCE. Why else the dreams of her skull split in two by an axe. Her foot caught in a bear trap. Her car going off a cliff. All those lovely images lived happily in my head.

But enough drifting off into my own troubles. It's J. Milton's life I'm trying to sort out here.

I called J. Milton Smith at the jail. Within a half an hour he returned my call. I don't know how the message got to him or even if he is allowed phone calls at will.

"Hey, Barbara Black. What's zup... have you found my killer for me yet? Can you save my ass, Lady? This being locked up with a bunch of whiney, I didn't do it, complainers... beginning to irritate me."

"Well, no. I am looking. And I need to see you. Tomorrow? And is there a good time to visit?"

"Yeah, lady, we're like the zoo. Open from nine to five. Come see the animals. I'm the striped one in the first cage to the left when you open the jail house door. Come see me. I'll get permission to talk to you. Or can we do it on the telephone? Answer the questions, I mean?"

"Nope. I've got a photo to show to you. Can't do it on this kinda phone. Can't do it anyway cause the pic is not on my phone and I don't have the technical know how to get it there. And besides, my "I don't like it here, friend" you only have a land line where you are. Let's you and I meet."

"Okay, but I reserve the right to stare at your tits."

I hung up. Why was I trying to save this jerk? Easy answer. For the money, the money, the money.

eleven

The next morning found me heading for the jail again.

This was becoming a Tuesday morning habit, too depressing for Monday mornings which already made me sad. Monday, the beginning of the work week. When I was young and had a job that I didn't much care for, seeing Monday roll around always brought me down. Then there were the years married to John. Oh how, I loved Mondays then. He went to work. I slept in, rose at a sunny nine-thirty and had a leisurely breakfast and planned what I would wear to dinner that night.

Perhaps marriage is a form of prostitution. I'm just thinking out loud. Don't call girls just have to worry about what to wear when they go out with their johns. High priced call girls I'm talking here. Perhaps that is what marriage to John was all about. I slept in, had a leisurely day, and at night we went to dinner, had a few drinks, came home and as they say, in marriage terms' 'made love.' Sometimes after John fell asleep, I got up and read for a while, watched a little TV, painted my nails. To tell the truth, I was a little bored, and maybe he was too. Now that I was scrambling around for every nickel, I was a little less bored, and a lot more productive. Maybe that was the answer. Maybe JOYCE came along to save me from a life of discreet boredom. If so, I should be grateful. But I still had a strong urge to strangle her with her own long blonde hair, whenever I thought of her. If she rescued me, I was apparently not quite yet at the point of gratitude.

However, I *was* at the point of arriving at the Pima County Jail. I was tempted to ask for an interview with the animal in the first cage to the left as you enter the main building, but I decided that might not amuse the deputy that would allow me to see J. Milton Smith. So I dutifully filled out the visitation form, walked once again through the metal detector, along the path of the sally port and after buzzing myself into the interview area, was assigned a new cubicle in which to meet my client.

J. Milton Smith entered his side of the room looking a little less haughty than he had sounded on the phone yesterday. He wasn't talking about anybody's tits today. As a matter of fact, discussions of anatomy seemed off the agenda.

"So whadayawant to see me about? You got something to show me, show!"

I held up the picture of his former wife Sally with the tall, rather good-looking bloke who I longed to put a name to.

"Don't know him. Never saw him before. Looks like they might have had something going, don't it? But still I don't know him. "

"No clue, huh?"

"Look, you're supposed to be the lady with the clues. You figure it out. And soon! Get me out of this place. A lot of these guys seem to be vying for my affections, and in a way I don't want. So, your job is to get me the hell out of here. Before they find a way to forcefully make me queer. You get the picture?"

"Question, so how come you aren't out on bail?"

"Dunno. Some idiot judge decided I was a flight risk. He set bail too damn high for me to qualify for it. Even at ten percent of it. Ask that not-so-smart child-lawyer of mine. If I hadn't given you a down payment it woulda jolly well helped me make bail. That much I do know."

"Okay. I got a few questions for you first, then I'll talk to your lawyer."

"Lay 'em on me."

"Your house. It's not exactly brimming with life, vitality, a sense of warmth, of home. Was this new or did you guys almost always live like one might occupy a hotel?"

"Nah. She wasn't into home décor. And not either one of us spent much time there. It is bare bones, I know. So what?"

"Well, it just gave me the idea that maybe what you had wasn't a big 'love match.' Was that always or just lately?"

"A marriage of convenience. Happened when I hadn't known her too long. Both of us in our senior year of college. She thought she was pregnant, and she was. I was there the night she miscarried. But it was too late. We were married by then, so we just went on with it. Her parents, see, religious zealots. She claimed they woulda killed her if she turned up pregnant and unmarried and when I met them, I believed it! And abortion, out of the question as far as she was concerned." He thought for a moment. "Me too, I think, the idea appalls me, though not for religious reasons, I just don't like it. It was my child too. I was sad when she lost it."

Almost as if embarrassed by being caught in an emotional moment, his tone of voice became brusque."

"So, as I said, we got hitched. As I got to know her better turns out she was kinda a bitchy sorta person. A little mean! We woulda eventually ended it, I think. But until recently neither one of us seemed to want out. She mentioned divorce a couple of times in the last few months. We were casually talking about who would get what, and then this. Somebody pops her."

"That is one way to end a marriage."

He ignored my comment and went on with his story. It sounded a little rehearsed to me, but he had had a long time to think about it.

"We knew there wasn't much of a stigma in society, or really even in the teaching profession anymore, against divorce. We just lacked the drive to complete or even start the legal stuff. And we sure as hell were in no mood to pay lawyers big amounts of money."

"Okay," I said. "That gives me a feel for things. I'll try other ways to figure this out. Who this guy is; how she met him; where she met him? Not a brother or a relative of any kind?"

"If she looked at a brother like that there would have to be an inquest about incest. Nah, I just don't know who the guy is. But nobody looks at a sibling like that, Lady. Unless they are truly amoral. How about you, Lady? You full of brotherly love? You kinky?"

"Let me remind you once again, Smith. These discussions we have. They are not about me. They are about you. We're trying to figure out who killed your wife. That's the focus. Try to remember that!"

He shrugged his shoulders. They didn't seem so broad in the orange jumpsuit.

He stood up and then remembering the protocol sat down again. "See ya." That was all he said. He turned his head away from me, folded his hands and looked down avoiding further interaction. I can take a hint. The interview had not produced much if any help for his cause and I rather imagine he sensed that. As I turned to leave, he raised his hand as if contemplating giving me the finger again, took a sly glance around and saw a deputy approaching and turned his gesture into a wave, but I had a feeling he would have preferred to signal his parting with a one finger salute.

twelve

Back to square one. No help there. I hadn't seen any tell-tale signs that J. Milton recognized the man in the photo, and just didn't want to share information with me. I don't think he knew who he was at all. I think I need to contact the lawyer. Find out from the fourteen-year-old very junior attorney why he had been unable to get bail set for his client.

Flight risk, lack of funds, bail set too high to meet even the ten per cent that bail's bondsmen required. The chances of me collecting on my bill, seemed even riskier than before.

Meanwhile I'd better make another appointment to check in with Ruth Ginsberg. No, I know, not the Supreme Court justice, the other one. She might talk me to death again, but if anyone outside of immediate family might recognize this guy it would be her.

When I got home, I was so enervated by the unsuccessful attempt to have a meaningful interview with my client that I decided a nap was in order. I was almost asleep when the phone rang, incessantly it would seem. Lacking caller ID, I had to answer it.

"Hello," I said sleepily, "This had better be important!"

"Well, I think it is."

It was the voice of my ex on the other end of the line. I sat abruptly up in bed.

"Well, what in hell do you want? Do you and JOYCE want to invite me to dinner? Let's all be buddies kinda thing. A little late I'd say."

"No, Just me. And dinner yes. How about we dine at Ventana Canyon Resort. You can meet me there. In the bar off the main entrance at about six-thirty if you're willing. Run a tab till I get there. I might be a little late."

"What's this about?"

"Let's talk about it tonight."

"Okay," I said, "Okay. I'll be there and, I'm a little thirsty, so you might not want to show up too late."

"See you."

What could John want of me, I mused. Maybe JOYCE moved out, or is preggers and he wants to name the kid after me, or he's tired of paying my severance pay and wants to make me a deal I can't resist to end it? Cash payout? I'd go for cash.

My thoughts switched to more practical matters. A haircut first and then a manicure and what should I wear? What did I have to wear that looked like Ventana? In our married days when we'd gone there, frequently I might add, I'd found that the very rich and those appeared to be most of the patrons, did not dress up at all. Especially not for the bar.

I chose a simple black dress from my closet, simple jewelry too as that was all I had on hand. I'd pawned some, but not all, of the good stuff to pay my lawyer at the time of my divorce. And that had worked out well! Ha!

I located a pendant with a knot displaying at the end of small gold links, jewels, fakes naturally, in all the colors of the rainbow.

Fortunately, I had found the missing matching earring in the bottom of a shoe the day before. Don't ask me how it got there. I drop things, all right! I had saved its partner in the hopes that one day again the missing part of the pair would show up.

I made a quick brush stroke or two to my shoes. Picked up the phone and called my manicurist hoping that she still remembered me and had not taken umbrage at the crummy tip I left her the last time I saw her. Called my hair salon, hoping a similar hope and ended up with two appointments in the early afternoon that could be managed quite easily if I drove a hundred miles per hour between the two.

Five-thirty found me dressed and pacing my small living room. I looked good, girl. One thing I wasn't going to have happen was for John to feel sorry for me. I thought about leaving later and springing for valet parking and realized I could leave now, save the valet parking money and arrive right at six-thirty after a hike from the parking lot that only somewhat resembled the journey up from the bottom of the Grand Canyon.

The drive is always pleasant, especially the winding 'guest's only' road that leads up the canyon to the parking area. It was only six when I got there. I locked my car, knowing full well that for miles on either side of me were cars that would be chosen over mine by any thief but a moronic one.

I arrived at the large double glassed doors only just a little out of breath. Entering I found quite a few patrons in the spacious bar area. A sign announcing that the George Howard band, whose mellow sounds I was acquainted with, would begin playing at eight. I had to wonder if I'd still be there.

There are three or four sections to the bar. Big square tables near the area where the band would play, a separate large group of tables that gave access to the viewing area for a huge wall sized TV where later the U of A football team could be watched by hopeful but oft disappointed locals. And there was the long bar itself with a couple of dozen stools, about the length of half a football field, and smaller tables near it.

I opted for a quiet corner table near the dance floor and ordered a Cuba Libre, my go to drink. The lighting there was flattering. Tall floor lamps cast a gentle glow on the tables. There were boxes of lights too, high up near the ceiling whose pleasant illumination filtered down on the scene below. There were attractive men and women sitting around. A couple in tennis outfits, a young woman, well youngish like me, staring intently at the screen of a tablet, reaching with the hand not on the keyboard for her drink. There were a couple of casually clad men talking with their hands about something I couldn't quite catch.

Suddenly, I caught myself wondering if John would show up. Was he annoyed enough at me over the divorce to set me up for a meeting and then just not show up? My stomach began to tie itself into knots. To distract myself from the sudden sensation of fear of the bar tab, which was quickly turning into nausea, I looked around the room.

I had noticed a bunch of Harley hogs in the driveway when I walked in. You could spot their owners almost immediately. Almost all of the women had a few tattoos, some wore hard looks and had loud, strident voices, but not all. The men, some with bandannas wrapped tightly around their foreheads, were in typical biker garb, leather pants and the like, though not all were dressed that way. As the evening progressed, I noticed couples joining them that looked more like dentists and their wives, or lawyers or doctors, maybe even an occasional real-estate magnate. After all that's the group that can afford Harleys these days.

I took a sip of my drink. Where was John? Again, the fear that he might stand me up. My trust level was sadly lacking, divorce does that to you especially when you've been replaced by a younger version of yourself.

The good news was that the waiter had not asked for payment, so I didn't volunteer. When I looked up across the length of the room, John was there. Dressed for the office, looking like a million dollars as he always did. He took long strides and reached my table.

"May I?" he said as he pulled out the chair next to mine.

thirteen

For a second it was just like old times. Happy husband, happy wife meeting after a day where he had made tough decisions as he climbed the corporate ladder, and I had made tough decisions as to how to spend my time and his money with as little effort as possible. Ah, the life I left behind.

That lasted only a second providing a moment of pure pleasure as I reflected on a lifestyle of total leisure. Was that all he meant to me? A puzzle to put aside and think about later.

"So, what's the purpose of this meeting, unless of course you just missed my blue eyes..."

"Same old Barbara. Let's get right to the point. Now! No 'Hi, how are you?' from this one, is there?"

"Nope, quite frankly, my dear, I don't give a damn."

"Conversation by movie quotes, you don't change much."

"I prefer to think my quotes are literary, but then you don't read much. Some things never change, you just swapped mates not habits."

"And that leads to what I want to talk to you about. Any chance I could get a drink first. The waiter is approaching, and this subject is a little difficult. I could use some bottle courage."

"Yes, of course, since you're paying. You are paying, right?"

"Yes, believe it or not I still do and always did have some gentlemanly instincts. But let's not go there because you will just want to remind me of how ungentlemanly I was in our parting."

As, John turned to address the now hovering waitress, a smiling young woman in a well-fitting white blouse, and black slacks, I said. "No, that's ground we've already covered. No point in revisiting it, is there?"

John made eye-contact with me and gave a quick shake of his head. That gave me time to realize that my hopes for a 'dear Babs take me back' scenario wasn't going to happen. I'd never really believed whole heartedly that a reunion was in the making, but some small part of me had hoped it. That part would now have to die the natural death of expectations not met.

John ordered a double martini with two olives which led me to believe he was not only thirsty but also maybe hungry enough to buy me dinner. That of course was what he had suggested. I no longer felt certain of his promises and I was exceedingly hungry. I was also well aware that if I didn't eat something soon, the generously rum infused drinks might not work in my favor were I to attempt to stand and leave the room. Wisely I realized that if I were to go for a dramatic departure, I might well fall on my face.

Nonetheless, when the waitress asked if "the young lady would have another," I nodded.

John turned back to face me. His eyes glowing in his darkly handsome face.

"So, how's the 'peeping tom' business going anyway?

I let that go.

"So far so good. One main client who's accused of murdering his wife. Sometimes I think he did do it. But no, somewhere out there is a guilty party and I've made some progress, but still looking for a witness who knew and yet liked this horrible woman. Lots of people were superficially acquainted with her but didn't know enough about her to know what was really going on in her life. Lots more who merely came across her from time to time seemed to have despised her. Obviously, not a well-liked woman. It's a long way from a solution."

"That's too bad."

I noticed John was listening to me with the same intensity he had given when I regaled him with accounts of my days of shopping for adornments of one kind or the other for my body. In short, he was apparently thinking about something else while pretending to listen to me, nodding every now and then. I considered beginning to recite the Nicene creed or the Gettysburg address just to test him. See if he'd keep on nodding until I grew quiet. Instead, I stopped talking.

"So, could you use another paying client?"

"It goes without saying, Yes, oh yes!"

"Well here's what I need from you…"

He paused while the waitress sat another drink in front of me and, in front of him, a vodka martini, as requested, in an old-fashion glass with two green olives glistening in the icy mix.

"Bring us dinner menus please." I breathed a sigh of relief and took a sip of my drink.

The waitress scurried off and he, knowing I hung on his every word, picked up where he had left off.

"It's simple really. Joyce wants to have a baby. I'm for fatherhood, I guess. Whatever makes her happy. I know we never talked about it, having children. I didn't really want to then, and you never said. Maybe we just thought it would happen, but it didn't… anyway, enough about the past."

Yes, I thought, dear God, enough about the past.

"Thing is Joyce never talks about her parents or siblings. Really not about herself much at all. Us, she talks about us, incessantly. How happy she is etcetera, etcetera, etcetera. When I ask about her family she always replies, using the same identical words as a matter of fact.

"She says, 'I don't have anything to do with them anymore. We've lost touch and I'd like to keep it that way.' She won't budge from that. I even asked her if she wanted more than one child.

"I was an only, as you know. So, I said, 'I'd like to have two kids, if we're going to have any. I think every child needs a sibling or even two. Did you have brothers and sisters?'

"Her response, 'Let's have the first one and then we'll see.' No response to my question. So, here's how it is. I married the woman. That's okay, but if I'm going to have children with her, I'm not taking chances that any monkey out of the barrel will do. I want to know about this family thing and pretty quickly. How is two-hundred dollars a day and expenses and if she never finds out about the research there is a bonus too. So, you have to be discreet."

"This is not in lieu of what you owe me according to our divorce decree, is it?"

"Of course not. How do you think that makes me feel? As if I would try to pull that one on you. Really, Babs?"

"Just checking. Yeah, I'll do it. Here's what I need. Her social security numbers. Any documents you have. Like when you got the marriage license, did she use a birth certificate or anything that you have a copy of? Also, her first, last and middle. I know nothing about JOYCE except for her first name. Nothing. You need to give me all of the info you have."

At that moment, the waitress reappeared and handed us each a three-page menu in an impressive looking black-leather folder and walked away. They had steak, so I ordered the filet mignon looking forward to the 'to go box' as much as to the meal itself.

We talked as we waited for dinner. Actually, John talked, and I listened. Mostly about his work, and about the work he was having done on what had been my much-neglected back yard. Then the band came on and we listened appreciatively to the mixture of jazz and a little bit of rock and roll. We'd both enjoyed live music and this band was superb and so we passed the time, alternately chewing and listening, until the check came.

John glanced at the bill, threw down a credit card. Gave me his most charming smile.

"I'll mail you what info I have. Oh, and a five-hundred-dollar retainer, if that suits you. You keep me up to date. You can call me but only at my office. You don't want to talk to Joyce, now do you? And I don't want her to yammer on about me being in touch with you, either. Lucy, my secretary now, middle-aged and grey haired, just the kinda help you always wanted me to hire, she'll put you through or give me a heads-up to call you back. Now, had I hired Lucy earlier on... maybe you and I would be talking babies, and I already know everything I need to know about your screw-ball family." He chuckled at what apparently to him was a joke. I let it go. I was salivating at the thought of a five-hundred-dollar check and did not want to offend the man who would be writing it.

"I'll mail you a check every Wednesday for as long as this takes unless you tell me differently. Like you're finished and have my answers, or you haven't had much time for my needs because of this murder thing. But I will tell you sooner is better. Apparently, my little Joycie has been on the pill and wants to wait at least six weeks before we begin trying for the wonder baby. That leaves me in condom hell, or celibate, so let's see if you can't give me what I need before I decide if I want to mix my genes with Joyce's."

"I have to ask. Why me? Why not some other PI?"

"Think about it. Someone else picked at random might find out stuff to blackmail us with. And besides the sooner you're successful, the sooner I can rid myself for the guilt of having cheated on you. Get real. This is more about what I need than how you feel!"

Same old John.

When the check came, he scribbled a signature, and stood. He pulled his wallet out of his back pocket. Replaced his credit card in it. Leaned over and planted a quick peck on my forehead, weaved his way through the dancing couples, and vanished.

Hmm, I thought, maybe JOYCE has some kick-ass bad hillbilly relatives and I'd get John back. But no, money and steaks, cuba libres and all, if I honestly assessed the encounter we had just completed, he had begun to bore me in just one evening's interaction. His dark handsomeness still intrigued me and there were memories stirred up of his warm embrace and let's face it sexual competence, but conversationally he was always mostly about dear old John himself. I should give old JOYCE a fair shake. There was a sense of power though. Imagine I could dictate, to some degree, whether or not they, JOYCE and John, had sex or at least whether or not he got to enjoy it. I wasn't having any. Maybe I could make his sex life miserable for just a while. That thought gave me a little internal grin.

I lingered for a moment or two more, remembering what it had been like to be part of a couple, before I shook myself free of reverie and proceeded towards the long walk down the incline to find my car. John, in all fairness to him, probably thought I had availed myself of valet parking and so was not totally lacking in manners in his failure to see me to my car.

The sparkling lights of the city would have been mine to enjoy if I hadn't had to keep my eyes peeled for a wandering rattler on my long dark route downhill, wondering how well I could run away from what I considered my natural enemies, snake or bob cat say, in extremely high heels. Gratefully, I was reunited with my car. On the trek down the mountain I wondered what I could do for the couple of days it took to get John's information. Couldn't I move forward in the matter of John Milton Smith? Better not confuse my Johns. And that provided me with my last chuckle for the day.

fourteen

I went to bed in my snuggly pjs. And dreamed, as I knew I would, of John and our days of seemingly endless pleasure. I woke with a smile on my face, immediately recognizing that coffee and reality were called for. Sure, I would have preferred orange-juice, tea or even a cold coke but none of that was to be found. So, coffee tempered with reality it was.

In the cold light of morning I could see that there was a lot on my plate. Except of course for breakfast. Empty on top, bottom and middle shelves my refrigerator reflected back into my eyes its blindingly white interior. I would have gone out for a celebratory breakfast but none of my potential income was sitting in my bank account, so I made toast from some stale bread, ate it without the benefit of margarine or butter, and might I add, without the benefit of clergy either as it was, I observed, a Sunday morning.

Over my coffee sans cream, the way lots of people like it, but I don't since I have a tendency to have two-thirds cream and little coffee, I tried to think of a way to stir up some real action on the case of the murder of Sarah Jane aka Sally Smith. Time to call RG again, only skip the B. If this Ruth Ginsberg had a middle name, I didn't know it. B for blabbermouth might be good. But then she'd not indicated her middle initial, and besides a blabbermouth is an advantage when you're seeking information. I needed to learn to appreciate her.

She had left me a number to call and so I punched in the digits, rubbing my ear in advance to begin circulation which I knew would not last long.

The call went to voice mail. I left a message. "Hello. (A good start, I thought.) This is Barbara Black, the woman who is investigating the murder of Sally Smith. I have a few more questions for you if you..."

"Hi, Ruth Ginsberg here. I was just screening my calls. Good to hear from you, I guess. Where has your curious mind led you?"

"I'm trying to find anyone, sister, brother, mother who might also know Sarah Smith fairly well, and if not currently at least in the past."

"There *is* a sister who lives here in town. On the far east side, I think. Don't think they were in anything like constant communication, as Sally woulda told me. After all, if she told me about her affair then I think she told me most every thought that crossed that mind of hers. And she had a good mind. Don't think she really liked teaching. She shoulda gone into business or something where she worked with adults, but maybe not in sales as people didn't instantly take to her. Again, for some reason I couldn't see. People said she was abrasive, but not me. I didn't think so. I thought she was swell."

Finally, Ginsberg seemed to run out of breath, so that I could ask another question.

"Can you give me a name for that sister. I'm sure my client could, but he's been a little surly lately. Not cooperative at all. Not like you. But then you're not wanted for murder." Ginsberg ignored my comments.

"Well, yeah, I can give you a little. Her sister's married name was Bournemouth, I remember because it was spelled Englishy with an 'e' and not like I would have spelled it B u r n m o u t h and of course the name itself is kinda different. Her name also began with an S, Suzanne... a French spelling for her first name, and she married a Brit sounding guy. That must have made for some interesting conversations about life on the continent. Whatever, I think he had an import/export store somewhere downtown. I think his name was Ian. I dunno, that's all I remember. Her folks were dead. And Ian and Suzanne had no kids either. Sort of a barren family. If she had any other close relatives, I didn't hear about em. Come to think of it, Suzanne and her British husband, they may have called it quits. I don't quite remember how that all worked out."

Again, Ruth Ginsberg had gotten to an end of her paragraph. I had stepped outside after writing down the info she gave me. In my apartment that is only a matter of two or three steps, and I rang the doorbell.

"Ooops! That's my door. Gotta go. Can I call you back?"

"Sure, but I don't know what else I can tell you. I'll be thinking about it."

"Okay, thanks, goodbye."

I gratefully hung up with just a moment's regret that I'd already used my best ploy for getting the hell off the line. What would I come up with next time?

fifteen

I turned on my computer and went looking for an Ian Bournemouth and sure enough found one. I found him to be the proprietor of Simply English, an import company apparently focusing on English imports, from teas and 'biscuits' to furniture. The address indicated the warehouse district right off Broadway just before going through the tunnel to downtown. Business hours included open on Sunday.

I took a quick shower and prepared to visit the store. Called Jane to see if she could go with me. Checked my purse to see if I could find enough ones and change to buy some imported tea, at least one bag's worth, and got in my car to pick up Jane.

A half an hour later, Jane asked, "So why are we doing this? Just what do you hope to accomplish by appearing first as a customer, albeit a cheap one, and secondly as an investigator?"

"Guess I hadn't thought that through. I just kinda wanted to meet him and maybe his wife, Sally's sister. Maybe she'll also work in the store on a weekend. That's why you're along, to maybe give me some idea of how my next approach should work. Do they seem like, well, nice people? Would they want to talk to me or anyone? Do they seem like people who could murder someone? Sometimes you can tell a lot in a seemingly accidental meeting, an exposure that no one deems as significant in any way. Course it will then take some 'splainin to do, Lucy' when it turns out I want to get information from them about Sally's cheatin' habits."

"And, so... you'll explain yourself and your interest in them how?"

"If I knew the answer to that then I wouldn't have to make this excursion. Just observe and both of us will try to remain somewhat inconspicuous, and then, later on, I'll try to find a way to meet the sister. Didn't remember her name, and if you see anything, a brochure or a business card, you grab it and put it in your purse, and we'll see if we can garner any additional info that way. Okay, my assistant sleuth? I simply have to play this one by ear, honest or not. I dunno. Just be so kind as to follow my lead and keep your eyes and ears open. I want to see what you think of him or them, too."

With some difficulty I made the left hand turn off Broadway onto Park and found myself hunting the number for the small shop. The storefront was so narrow that only the initials showed up over the door of the establishment. A large S separated from the letter E by the flag of Great Britain sat above the narrow doorway. Inside the less than pristine surface of glass was a sign that read 'open'. Beneath that was a clock that could be arranged, it was cardboard after all, to read a specific time under the words Back in... minutes. It was not currently in use.

The bell on the door jingled when I opened it. A tall man, somewhat stooped and obviously at least middle-aged, stood behind a dusty, glass fronted counter. The walls were covered with framed pictures and plaques. Pictures of boats on the Thames, castles surrounded by moats, the London bridge that everyone knew and loved which was really Tower Bridge, which many Americans confused with London Bridge. (The real London Bridge actually now hangs out in Lake Havasu, Arizona. Either we bought it from the Brits. or they gave it to us, I can't remember. I think maybe a McCulloch bought it.)

There were also photos of Queen Elizabeth and of course one or two of Diana also graced the walls. There was a rack of imported English teas, and food stuffs near the front door. The back of the room held antiques which to my eye did not indicate they were of British origin, but most probably were.

A rather gaunt gentleman came out from behind his counter. He smiled in an expression that did not reach his otherwise world-weary eyes. He didn't look like a young Robert Redford, he looked like the older version.

"May I help you find something in particular?" he asked.

"I love all things English. Been described by my friends as an absolute Anglophile. But I'm here today attempting to locate the sister of Sarah Jane Smith. I'm Barbara Black. A private investigator. I represent her husband, the man accused of murdering her. And I am trying to get a handle on who Sarah was before I decide to believe, or not, his cry of innocence. I understand your wife is Sarah Jane's sister." So much for deception, I thought, as I blurted out the whole unvarnished truth.

"My ex-wife to be exact. We've been divorced for approximately six months now. But I am in contact with her. I'll give you her number and you can call her."

The proprietor of this quiet establishment walked back to his counter. There were no other customers and I had to wonder if the middle of a Sunday afternoon might be a time when the lack of buyers indicates an almost over-whelming clue to an unsuccessful business venture.

"Perhaps you would be kind enough to let your ex know that I'll be calling her." I glanced up at him anxious to make eye contact to show my sincerity.

"I get hung up on a lot in my business. Like to avoid that when I can. Meanwhile, could I get a look at that small chest of drawers. I'm furnishing a new place, myself. I'm also recently divorced." I sent in his direction, a quiet sad commiserating sort of smile hoping that I would ingratiate myself enough to form the beginnings of mutual respect and possibly even a friendship.

I wanted him to think, if possible, 'Us divorced people got to stick together.' After all, if his wife, ex-wife that is, didn't want to speak to me, perhaps he would. And in-laws often were much more ready to 'dish the dirt' on someone more so than a person who was related to and therefore often sympathetic with a relative or just bent on protecting the family name.

Ian started to speak again.

"That chest, young lady, is quite valuable. Still I've had it for a long time. I might be able to let go of it for, say... four-hundred dollars." He seemed less old now as he warmed to a favorite subject, English furniture. He became more animated, stood straighter and now seemed somewhat handsome and mysterious. His blue eyes twinkled in an unlined face and I found myself beginning to enjoy our interchange. He was wearing a muted-plaid shirt which displayed a chest not at all given to fat, no man boobs, thank God. I despise man boobs. He had on grey slacks and a pair of loafers without socks, tastefully but modernly dressed. I, for one, liked what I saw.

After a pause for assessment of the man and his chest (both kinds), I said.,

"It was a good idea. But you're about two-fifty above my comfort zone." I tried to keep my expression and tone of voice, light and bantering.

"Why don't we meet in the middle? Say two-twenty-five.

I smiled. "Make that two hundred and I could pick it up on Wednesday. I won't have the money in my account until then."

"Wednesday, then. In the afternoon. I don't open until two p.m. But I could meet you here earlier. Especially if you were available for lunch, say. Then, afterwards, I could help you load it into your car."

I'd wandered over to the chest. It was beautiful. Mahogany with tile inlaid in the center of its top surface, and absolutely gorgeous marble pulls on the drawers. I opened a drawer to be sure it didn't stick.

"You have yourself a deal". I smiled shyly up at him. Perhaps I had made a friend.

Jane had been standing next to me in the front of the store. I had inconsiderately left her there, alone and unsmiling, watching the little tableau that unfolded.

The proprietor, who I now judged was not as much of an antique himself as I had initially surmised, was busy taping a small, red, 'sold' label to one of the drawer-pulls carefully avoiding placing anything sticky on its wooden surfaces.

"This is my cousin, Jane," I said, quickly finishing the formal business of an introduction. "And you can call me Barbara, since we're going to have lunch soon."

This time the smile went all the way to his eyes.

"Ian, Ian Bournemouth here. Fine, can we meet here on Wednesday and then go to lunch. There is an English tearoom just up a few blocks on Broadway. They buy a lot of stuff from me and I try to return the favor. So, no arguments. Lunch will be on me. Say, eleven-thirty on Wednesday?" He turned slightly toward Jane. "Will you join us, young lady?"

I admired his inclusion of her.

Jane said, "No, I'm not available due to work. But thanks."

Ushering Jane ahead of me, I turned back to Ian. "See you Wednesday, I won't be late." And I followed Jane out of the room, through the door and down the porch stairs, toward my car.

In my car, with the doors barely closing, Jane asked.

"What's with you and an antique chest of drawers? I wouldn't think you could afford it."

I nodded. "You're probably right. Just an impulse buy. I am so careful with my money; just every now and then I need to splurge a little. And it's almost time for my severance pay from dear old John to hit the bank. I'll be spending some of that."

Jane shrugged her shoulders.

She asked, "What did you do with the phone number for Sally Whatsits sister?"

I shifted gears and pointed to the side pocket of my purse. Jane retrieved the small square of paper from its interior, amazed that she could find anything on a first try.

"Better not lose this one. You gonna use it right away?"

"I dunno. I'll have to think about it. What you think?"

"I'd hold off. Meet with him first. Let him think you'd rather hear what he thinks before you interview the wife. That would be my bet. Say, you're not hung up on this old guy, are you? He's old enough to be your uncle. But I got to admit, it was gentlemanly of him to include me in the invite, even though I could tell it was you he wanted to drag off into an English tearoom and devour."

"Nope, I'm not hung up on him. But he seems nice. And I could use a friend. It's lonely out here in divorce land and you are about the only person I see. He seemed lonely too. So, I'm cultivating him for two reasons. Oh, and a third, I really am an Anglophile!"

"Okay cousin of mine. Seems like an odd choice for a playmate, but I guess you know what you're doing. Just watch out. The ole letch wants to meet you in his closed business. Probably innocently but..."

"I'm sure I can handle the situation, but thanks for your warning. Your trust level seems to be low, however. I'm just saying..."

"It's men. Men in general. Like your John. He seemed such a good guy. Well he didn't seem to like me much and he is ego-centric to the extreme, but he seemed to be on the straight and narrow. And then the Joyce thing. I mean really. And my experience with men. Ugh. They appear to like me till I stand up and start to walk away and then the limp gets 'em every time. I'm not unattractive and rather clever in conversation. At least I think so. And then nothing. The only men that flirt with me are often the parents of the kids in my classroom, the *married* ones. Ugh, men!"

Had I turned over a rock and found another Ruth Ginsberg? Jane had delivered her diatribe about men in paragraph form, and seemingly kept talking until she ran out of breath. Here's hoping my new friend and shall I say admirer, Ian, would be capable of brief exchanges of conversation.

When we reached Jane's neighborhood, she said, "That's it for me today. Laundry awaits. I'll just take my lousy mood home with me. Thanks, anyway. No time for lunch today."

"Listen, after I see Ian on Wednesday you and I can re-hash that encounter. Dinner Wednesday night on me. And I don't mean coupon dinner. I'll take you someplace nice."

"Deal." Jane got out of the car, gave me a tremulous smile and turned her back and walked quickly to her apartment door. I had the feeling she was ready for a good cry. Add to my to do list, if I ever met a decent, caring non-judgmental man, introduce him to Jane.

sixteen

When I got home, I found tucked between my screen and front doors a large manila envelope. Inside I found a note from John.

"This is all I could find. Hope it's enough to get you started."

I inserted my key into the door, flung my purse at the nearest chair and sat down on my crummy love-seat couch which was covered in one of those horrible plaids you find in cheap used furniture venues and had become mine for only fifty-six dollars and some odd change. The odd change I could and did find under the seat cushions

Still it was comfortable and mine. I slid my letter opener, which also served as a nail file, under the flap and lifted out the meager contents of the envelope. No official looking documents fell out.

Rather there was one page obviously typed, I'm assuming here, by John. It gave all the information he had acquired in reference to Joyce. It said,

"The birth certificate Joyce presented when we applied for our marriage license is missing from the file drawer in my home study. Truly I filed it under Joyce, birth certificate, so it would not be hard for her or anyone else to find. I remember this about it. She was born in Waco, Texas. Date of Birth December twentieth nine-teen-eighty-nine which would make her twenty-eight years old. She was christened or at least named Joyce no-middle-initial Kelleman. I did not read mother and father names or if I did, I've forgotten them.

"We've added her to my personal checking account. The social security number she used there was 563-72-*#^^." (I recognized John's code for those last four. We still had some secrets only the two of us shared, though come to think of it, maybe numerous other women were in on all our former secrets)

"We have not yet filed a joint tax return. Is the soc. real? I have no way of knowing."

John went on to say, "When she came to work for me, I hired her as a part-time secretary. Ostensibly she was to take over the front desk for Madeline at lunch times and when Madeline went on break or was in my office taking notes. She was also supposed to run errands from time to time. I interviewed her. I decided she would make the front desk look good.

"She asked to be paid off the books. Said there was an errant ex-husband who was trying to locate her and had the money to hire smart private detectives who could and would find her. I had my bookkeeper do just that. Pay her off the books. Hell, she wasn't an illegal. Just a part-timer. Didn't want or need benefits she said. That became true when I became her benefactor. She has since admitted to the lie of the ex-husband story. Said she made it up on the spot. Didn't want to fill out forms etc. etc. for a part-time job as she intended on her off time to look for something better. That is what she told me before we were married, and I believed her.

"This is all I got. I don't want to ask for more till we have some more facts to go on. See what you can dig up. And soon. When I look at what I do know, I don't know shit from Shinola, and I want to find out this stuff yesterday. Get on it. Prove you are a PI worth your salt. Go get 'em, Babs!"

The longer the note went on, the more I thought John probably dictated it to someone. Lucy, the new middle-aged secretary? Probably. Boy, was she ever privy to a lot of stuff. Or maybe he had a program on which he could dictate, directly, a lengthy treatise like this one. I'd seen John type. Hunt and peck and hunt some more. I doubted it was his effort involved in the actual preparation of the document. Not my John, my lazy John. But maybe a lot had changed about him that I didn't know. I might buy that he was no longer lazy. Well... no!

I moved over to my computer. Turned it on and waited for it to pop to life. The best angle seemed to me to be date of birth and location of same. This woman did not want to leave a paper trail. Yeah. That's suspicious in and of itself.

First, I Googled the Branch Davidians at Waco, Texas. Let's face it that is what Waco, Texas reminds almost every one of at first glance. But that standoff was in April of nineteen-ninety-three or rather ended there as the compound went up in flames that day. The dates didn't seem to be related to one another. And yet there were other children, three and four-year-old children one of which might have been JOYCE. A trip to Texas might be required to see if I could find out who, if any, of the Branch Davidian children had been taken away from the compound and settled elsewhere.

I decided I would look at official records for the hospital there and did. No record of the birth of a baby girl in the Waco General Hospital in December of nineteen-eighty-nine. Lots of mid-wifery in Texas at that time. Public records didn't show any mention of anybody named Kelleman. Close to Kellerman though. I checked that out. Nothing there either.

Another idea occurred to me. I texted John. Could he send me the address where JOYCE was living when they were dating? If dating is what you name a cheating couple's rendezvous, I wondered about that. Should I ask for where she lived when they were sneaking around or more specifically screwing around. Maybe, better not. He is a paying customer.

John texted back a mid-town address. I looked at it. Took a hot shower, put on a pair of clean pjs and flicked on the TV. A woman of action, that's me.

Monday morning dawned a gloomy and unwelcoming sight. I thought about staying in, lounging on the couch and waiting until Tuesday to face the prospect of functioning as a fully formed adult in a world where I had no lover, few friends and some job assignments that seemed at this point to belong to someone with far more capabilities than I possess.

Starving, and if you checked my refrigerator that would seem to be the only alternative to not leaving the house, led me to reluctantly put some clothing on, wash my face, brush my teeth and scramble around on the floor to find my other tennis shoe.

By eight-thirty, I was on the road. First the grocery store then a quick run by of the address that had been provided to me by John of the location of his fair JOYCE when she first decided to help him in his plan to cheat on me.

That's my assumption anyway, that she took one look at the handsome Johnny and decided he was fair game.

I drove to Alvernon and Speedway and surveyed the neighborhood. Cheap apartments everywhere. There was also a handy Fry's Grocers nearby, so I decided to shop first, discover later. I always kept in my car a handy insulated bag for the few occasions when I purchased groceries of any kind. My type of shopping today was based on three absolute necessities, spur of the moment, no plan, no coupons, toilet paper, cereal, and milk. Anything beyond that was someone else's idea of how to function successfully in modern society.

Inside the store I located the cereal aisle, chose something only a five-year-old would adore, found a carton of milk and the paper goods aisle and was almost through. The cold storage bins in the center of the aisle in the back of the store offered me additional inspiration. I chose orange juice, some cans of V-8, after all I was seeking a balanced diet, and a six-pack of diet Pepsi. Looking at the contents of my cart I diagnosed that I was more thirsty than hungry.

I balanced all this with a package of baloney, a block of cheddar cheese and a small jar of mayonnaise of an unfamiliar but cheap brand. There! Lunch and breakfast, quite an accomplishment.

Outside I found my car as I had left it, no car thieves this morning apparently, and I proceeded to place orange juice, some pulp, and baloney, cheese and milk in the insulated foil-lined bag. I noticed that lunch had become an iffy menu item. I had failed to purchase bread and vowed to find a bakery, later on this morning, that was close to home to get some good crusty bread. It would be too humiliating to go back into Fry's and stand in line again to buy a loaf of bread. I have my pride!

But first the apartment building and perhaps a manager who could remember JOYCE as after all she had only been gone less than a year. See how quickly she could foul up my life, I thought. Surely, she should be remembered for that alone. But then I realized the modern manager might not be required to know much about her tenants especially the ones who had already moved on. Turns out I was, thankfully, wrong about that.

There were many apartments to choose from, but the actual address took me to a small group of units sitting sidewise to the street. The sign said Garden Apartments. If there were 'gardens', they were not evident. Probably, the word 'garden' was because all the apartments were ground floor dwellings. A certain advantage as having no one above you eliminated the possibility that the owners of a pair of full-sized poodles could live on the second floor and shake your ceiling as dogs or elephants or whatever the semi-domesticated animals that always seem to live above you might be. They then proceed to jump off the furniture and onto the floor in a gay daily chase of one another round and round. Perhaps I exaggerate, but in one of my lifetimes in one of my apartment settings that was my experience. Okay, I'll admit it was dogs, not elephants, but in my over-active imagination, standard poodles can produce nearly as much noise and reverberations as baby elephants.

The last apartment in the row had a card marked Manager in the window. I knocked. A faded woman in a too-many-times washed housedress answered my knock. I held out my PI card. She took it, glanced at the info and said in a faint voice... "Yes ?"

"I'm making enquiries about JOYCE... "I hesitated, and the woman supplied in her listless way the word... "Barnes" and then said no more. I continued on with my interrupted thought... "who I believe lived here last year or so. Can you tell me if you remember her or anything in particular about her?"

"Yes, I could tell you..."

Reluctantly I held out a twenty that I had just released from my debit card for this week's foolishly expensive and expansive lifestyle and which I had planned to last me all the seven days for my pocket money to say nothing of my hope to appease my growling stomach with an egg-McMuffin this very morning.

With more alacrity than I expected the woman, who had otherwise seemed relaxed to the point of paralysis, snatched the bill out of my hand and thrust it into the pocket of her almost colorless dress.

"Yeah, she lived here. She kept her place neat. She dressed clean and went to work on the bus every day after she got a job. Her boss got to bringing her home. Then he got to picking her up in the mornings and then taking her to work and finally he just didn't leave. He stayed the night.

"The walls are pretty thin around here. Hers was the apartment next to mine. Right next door to where you're standing. They did a lot more foolin around than they did sleepin. Last I heard, he got divorced and married her. And, of course, they don't live here. He musta had some money 'cause he drove a nice car and dressed good. Don't know if he had a wife or not, but he does now... her!"

"Well, that sums it up. Thanks. Can you tell me how long she lived here and if she ever had any other steady company or a relative visiting or anything like that.?"

"She signed a two-year lease. And she broke the last six months of it, there was a penalty, but she paid it. So that puts her here about eighteen months. Never saw nobody else but the boyfriend and I saw a lot of him. But there was an Oklahoma license plate parked in her spot for about three weeks right after she first got here.

"You wait right there. I wrote down the number, the license number, didn't know if there was gonna be any trouble with someone. I never saw no one. Those last few days when the car was still there. And then I saw this girl. A child really. About fourteen years old, just beginning to look like a woman, and a boy looked somewhere between seventeen and nineteen like he must have just begun to shave. I was outside when they loaded up some luggage one day and then they was gone from here and so was the car."

The manager left the doorway, not closing it in my face but there was no suggestion that I might enter. She came back moments later with a small piece of paper. She opened the door long enough to thrust into my hand a hastily pencil-written note that said merely JHS4146 Oklahoma plate, expires November, twenty-sixteen. I wrote it down.

"Didn't know if I'd have to charge her for renting out some of her space. If they was going to stay with her for long, I'd had to charge her more rent."

"Thanks."

The woman gave me a nod. "That's all I got. Hope that helps. Bye." And the door closed almost as quickly as it had opened leaving me standing there with the note clutched in my hand, twenty dollars poorer but with some hope that I finally had a lead on the past life of JOYCE Barnes. Not Kelleman now but Barnes... wonder how JOYCE explained that discrepancy to my John or if she ever did.

And about this place. No telling how good a manager the woman was, but she sure knew how to pay attention to detail. Great for me. A bit of good luck. I observed the appearance of the rather run-down building. Not all gardens are Eden-like I said out loud as I walked away.

seventeen

Back home I got on the phone. I was blessed with a girlfriend who had been married to a friend of ours who had, guess what, left her for a younger model, a secretary of his... ah coincidence. She had ended up in Oklahoma City and worked for the Department of Motor Vehicles there. Occasionally, miracle of miracles, the fates converge, and a coincidence works for me instead of against me.

I called Martha at home. We began a lovely chat about the joys of divorce and singleness handed out generously to us by former mates who were generous in no other way. I got down to business at the end of our conversation and she promised to check out the license plate and let me know. Her job left her privy to the information and she could research a license plate for me. Course she'd have to assign the inquiry to an entity that could be billed so as not to risk her job doing it. Just by entering a company name that paid taxes in the state of Oklahoma, and she could think of one, she could request the information and then get the info to me. She'd have to give a copy to the company as well and someone would probably call her and ask what the hell is this all about and all she'd have to do is claim a mix-up, remove the fee, and then we'd have the info. It was something she did. A side-line she called it. Her job didn't pay all that well.

"Not a kind of mistake I can make too often. But it works for me if it works for you and I'll only charge your ex fifty dollars for it and then split it with you. I've got a blank invoice around here somewhere."

"Listen, pal make it seventy-five dollars and don't bother to split it. Send me the bill, and I'll see to it that Johnnie boy pays it. Believe me, he just wants results and he doesn't care what it costs. I'm here to be sure it costs aplenty. Seventy-five oughta buy you a decent dress to go out and carouse in. I think our exes owe us that, since carousing is their thing! Or was! Poor dear boys married the women who seduced them, or visa-versa. Don't know how often they are gonna play that game but, let's take little bits of advantage of their wayward ways when we can."

Martha said. "I'm in with that. Talk to you soon. Look for my bill, but first I'll call you or text the information I get."

"Great, girlfriend, and thanks."

I'd done what I could do for today. JOYCE Kellemen aka Kellerman aka Barnes was fixed in my sights and was going to get dealt with, yes! Monday had been put to good use and lunch with Ian was Wednesday's business.

Tuesday, I stayed home. Risked an encounter with the bra thief on the stairs to and from the laundry-room but saw no one. Paid some bills after I deposited the check that came in the mail from John and felt for the first time in a long time like I was solvent, or solventish, since the rent would be due next week. I had groceries, of sorts, a warm apartment, okay often too warm as the landlord controlled the thermostat, a checkbook with a balance with four zeroes if you count the ones after the decimal and I always do, and the opportunity to get endless information from several sources in the next few days. I was on top of my world for a change.

Wednesday dawned bright and clear as Tucson days, no matter the season, almost always do. I read the paper, had a cup of tea and a small bowl of Captain Crunch... I told you it was a five-year-old's choice... and looked at my options for what to wear to my lunch with Ian.

Everything I own was clean and hanging in the closet. Everything I own is not a hell of a lot.

I chose a pale lavender blouse with a white collar, my one pair of dressy pants and a rather smart looking gray blazer. I added actual dress-up shoes, flats though, in case I had to run away from Ian 'cause he didn't look like he could run really fast but you never know. Looks can be deceiving and Jane's idea that he could be the mad rapist had stuck in my mind. For a moment that idea rather appealed and then I shook myself and realized I needed to go out on a few dates, or I might go a little crazy.

I dressed in old clothes first and took my car to the local car wash. The three-dollar wash had gone from five and then to six dollars now and that really pissed me off. It was the same identical service I got last year for half the price. But, I did it anyway. I'll save my protests for the big things in life.

At least the vacuum cleaners were free, so I pulled over to the clean-up spot, emptied a yard of trash, old diet coke cups and candy bar wrappers out of the back where I had casually tossed them for the last three years and finally had a presentable vehicle. Time to go home to get properly made-up so that I could wend my way westward and meet Ian for lunch. Took a shower, tried on the lavender blouse, and other parts of my ensemble, matched earrings to them and carefully applied my makeup.

I seemed to remember that we were to meet at the shop and wondered if I should call Ian and request that we meet at the restaurant he had proposed for our lunch. Out of my far distant past I recalled the old rule of caution for a first date. Realizing I had no phone number for him, I gave up on that idea and set out for his place of business.

Ian's car was an old beat-up VW bug, not the new variety, I'm talking nineteen-sixties. The bug that probably should have been allowed to rest after all these years, sat lonely and forlorn in front of the door of the Simply English import store. I climbed the crumbling six steps to the porch landing and knocked tentatively at the door. I was wondering if Ian had adequate liability insurance in case a shopper fell on those stairs when the door was pulled open, and I stepped inside practically into the arms of my date.

Ian looked very spiffy today. He had on an ascot. Well, of course an ascot, he's English. It went well with the blue of his shirt. He was wearing Dockers, and boots, but thank God not of the cowboy variety and his handsome, long face barely suppressed excitement. Rather apparently, he was also looking forward to our luncheon *date* as was I.

He stepped out on the porch and locked the door behind him, set the 'back-in-a-minute' clock to reflect an hour and a half absence. He took me by the arm and gently guided me down the steps. Nice old guy, but I had to wonder in how many years I would be taking his arm and gently guiding... well never mind. You get the drift.

He observed my wreck of a car sitting next to his wreck of a car. Apparently, mine won the toss-up.

Ian had a suggestion.

"Why don't we take your car? It looks like yours will make it up Broadway for a mile or two and back down and with mine you can't be too sure. Ah, the joys of divorce from someone with a really good lawyer."

Ian smiled at his little joke and I smiled and nodded. We both knew it was a bit of irony that was too often true. When he smiled, he looked a lot younger, I thought. Maybe forty-five fifty in that range.

"She got the new Toyota and I got to keep this. All's fair in love and war, is the saying. But when love becomes war unfortunately it is not so."

I got my keys out of my purse without a lot of fumbling around.

"Listen, they're paid for aren't they, and we're obviously not car-proud kind of people. One more good character reference for us both. Not car proud. Suckers in other ways perhaps, but definitely not into showing off with our vehicles our admirable status in the community."

Ian chuckled.

He changed the subject.

"You'll like this place. It's not too tea and crumpets and fortunately not too into English cooking otherwise. You'll not find mashed overly sweet peas or a gravy that can only be described as tasteless and they do not boil liver here as they do in London's traditional English restaurants."

"Yes," I said. "I may be an Anglophile, but I won't starve for it."

"Way to go. Let's order like people who actually like food."

We were seated by a nice-looking older lady at a small table next to the front window. The menu presented some variety. True there was an endless list of English teas. Scones were on the menu and shortbreads and biscuits, which as we all know are really cookies, but the entrees were all of the American variety or at least international. Ian chose a ham and cheese sandwich with a side salad and carefully selected his tea. I had a large crisp salad that included bacon and avocado. The bacon was crisp as was the lettuce. Indeed, quite un-British in both appearance and taste. I added a cranberry scone for authenticity and went with the same tea as Ian had chosen, as he seemed to know best about that sort of thing.

While we waited for our meal an awkward silence set in. Then we both spoke at once.

"I suppose you'd like some information about my sister-in-law. Ian asked his question while simultaneously I asked, "Can you tell me a little about your sister-in-law?"

As our words and thoughts both over-lapped, we chuckled, and then Ian continued on.

"Sally, well really Sara Jane, was a lot like my wife. Confident, a little brassy, quite sure that she was right about everything. What I mean to say is overconfident and obnoxiously brazen, but my original statement seemed so much more proper."

"Hey, Ian, if we're going to be friends, and I for one hope we are, I need you to be willing to speak what's on your mind, not soften it up for me."

"Well, it's true. They both thought they knew more than they did about a lot of subjects. From politics to fashion. The best bet was to let them talk, not interrupt and for God's sweet sake, not correct either of them. Neither one of them took well to being setstraight on any subject. It turned me into a silent man, and, did rather the same for J. Milton. We snuck off from time to time to a pub, and never said much about it. But one time I do remember, both of us shaking our heads and commiserating with one another briefly as we tried to remember just what it was that had originally attracted us to our wives, the lovely all-knowing sisters.

I nodded again, to encourage Ian to continue but also in agreement. Marriage to a person of strong opinions, I'd been there.

"Actually, it was that they were sexually attractive women and coy and what you Americans might call *cute* at first. It took forever in my case to be disillusioned about the quality of life with Suzanne and in J. Milton's case not quite as long. Neither of us felt we could afford a divorce, that came up once or twice between us. And as it turns out, that was true!

I nodded. I was becoming a real bobble-head.

"If Milton chose this other way out of the marriage, and it appears he did, murder is somewhat extreme, I'd say, wouldn't you?"

I said,

"My hope and what I'm trying to prove is that Milton didn't kill his wife, your sister-in-law. He says he didn't, but meanwhile I'm trying to find out more about Sarah Jane, see if I can find anyone else who mighta wanted to do her in. Did you know if she was having an affair and that maybe it wasn't the first or only time?"

"No, I didn't. But my ex might have known. If she did, she would not have shared that information with me. It would depend on the timing of course. Years ago, she would have dished the dirt on her sister to me, but no, we've been estranged though living together still for years now. So, I may not be too much help. Sorry, if you're spending this time with me to find out more about Sarah. I don't know that much."

"Okay, Ian, I'll level with you. That was my original intent in looking you up. But, well, divorce is a lonely bit. I lost most of my friends in the community property split. Apparently, they were his and I didn't catch on until too late. So other than my cousin Jane, I don't see a lot of people. I thought, we might be friends."

"Oh, rather. I'd like that. I'll help you in any way I can with your inquiries, but then I'd like us to just talk. I, too, am as lonely as a pigeon lover in Trafalgar Square. I, too, could use a friend."

The conversation was getting a little too personal for the likes of me. I think actions speak louder than words and so was hoping we could just get back to being friends without talking about it. I changed the subject.

"I met the people at Sarah Jane's school. Other than one lone supporter, they didn't seem too fond of her. Actually, from what I could tell, other faculty actively disliked her. Did Sarah and Milton interact with friends of yours and did she make any contacts or bonds there that would seem to extend beyond those encounters?"

"Neither of the Brisconce sisters were good at making friends. Suzanne and I didn't have many. Acquaintances, yes. People I would qualify as friends, people who sought us out to go to dinner or to join in an activity. Not many if any. I have some friends from the business. Antique collectors like me. Suppliers of which there are a few. We meet from time to time for dinner or drinks or something. But as a couple, nil. We had none. The sisters, spoke on the phone, met for lunch infrequently. Even they didn't seem that enamored of one another."

"So, no sources. Okay. So, what do you do to amuse yourself?"

"I work. I read some journals about business. I poke around at estate sales trying to find authentic English pieces on the cheap. I work. No clerks. I'm there if the store is open and as you can see, it's not terribly busy these days."

"Are you like me and barely supporting yourself? And if so, I hope we'll be able to hang out over a cuppa tea. No frills in my line of work, at least not yet."

"You are actually a tea drinker? My, my that's pleasing."

"Iced tea, soft drinks, water... almost anything but coffee though from time to time even that. That probably makes me un-American, not being addicted to early morning coffee. I like to get up late too. And stay up late. Weird, huh?"

"The coffee bit maybe. Night owls are not exclusive to any country. I myself am an early riser and late go to bed type. I don't need much sleep. Matter or fact if I sleep too much, I worry that I am getting depressed. And on that subject, divorce from Suzanne has given me a new lease on life. Absent the daily, hourly and constant criticism, this skinny old Brit is beginning to feel pretty good about himself."

I acknowledged that divorce could and often does, to say the least, *lighten* one's self-esteem especially if you are not the divorce seeker.

"Well, maybe it's different for me," said Ian. "I sought the divorce, finally and after many years of what I can only presume was abuse. Not physical abuse. More mental, the constant downgrading of my feelings, my actions and my abilities. I will admit, a great cloud has lifted from my life. I like to call it, *Suzanne.*"

"Nice to name your clouds," I said. "Mine was named John. And JOYCE, my ex-husband's new hobby. She was the blackest little cloud of all."

We had finished our lunch and drunk our tea. We both stood and walked toward the door.

"Step outside into the sunlight with me, my dear. Things are looking up. At least that's what my new-found friendship with you seems like to me."

"Definitely, sunshine," I said.

I drove us back to Ian's shop. We were both pretty quiet on the short trip. No reason to be otherwise. A kind of contentment had set in. For me at least, I hoped it was so for Ian."

I said, "For the moment, here and now and in your presence, I feel pretty content, mellow as it were."

"Rather," Ian said. He dragged the word out as if he were the one with the southern drawl. An impressive word as he enunciated it.

At the shop, I gave Ian two-hundred dollars in cash. He handed back fifty of it. "Friends and relations price," He said.

"Okay," I said. "But here's the deal. Come Saturday night dinner is on me and you get to name the place."

"How lovely," said Ian. "Strangely enough, I love Mexican food. An unusual taste perhaps for a Brit, but there you are." We agreed on meeting at seven at my favorite Mexican food place, La Parilla Suisa. He smiled as he loaded the chest of drawers into my car.

We had separated the drawers from their base inside the store and somehow or another made all the parts fit into the back and front seats of my car. I stood on my tiptoes and planted a kiss on the dear man's cheek, and got into my car and drove away. In the rear-view mirror I saw him standing there, his hand on his cheek, looking like a happy man.

eighteen

What was I doing? He had to be twenty years my senior. But I have always been a fool for charm when accompanied by skill with the language. He sure had both of those. It wasn't like we'd sworn eternal fidelity to one another. Actually, we'd not had so much as a second date, if this could be counted as a first one. But I liked Ian. Liked how I felt when I was with him. Some dumb movie, part of the script, or a book... I'm not sure. What I remembered was the idea: "Love is how you feel when you're with someone" or something of that nature. I wasn't leading him on. I was enjoying being with him. For me that was enough. I hoped it was for him too.

Also, bless him. He had not insisted on or even hinted that he might accompany me home and unload the items. He wasn't pushy at all. And I liked that too.

Outside my apartment I began to wish Ian had offered to see me home. Getting this bulky and heavy item up to my apartment was going to present a challenge. I started with the smallest drawer. Inside the building I headed for the elevator. Second floor apartments have advantages over first floor ones. Not so easily broken into for one thing. But moving furniture in and out was not one of them.

At my door I set the drawer on its side, opened the door and took it inside, locked the door again as I left, and repeated those actions five times more until I was downstairs staring at the empty base of a chest of drawers wondering how in the hell I was going to move it. Even minus its drawers it weighed a ton.

The bra-thief or supposed bra-thief appeared at the front door of our apartment building. A quick thought to the impossibility of my getting help anywhere else left me saying what I thought I'd never say to *this guy*.

"Say, could you give a girl a hand. I gotta get this monstrosity up to my apartment. Do you think you could help me?"

His degree of startle showed in a deer-in-the-headlights look. My unnamed neighbor finally opened his mouth to speak.

"Well... sure... why not?"

We shared the elevator in silence, me wondering if he was a bad guy after all and him probably wondering where I got the nerve to ask for his help.

At my door, I said, "Thanks." Without a word he turned and walked off. Ah well, mission accomplished. Weird or not he had helped. Maybe he found it too awkward to talk to me, or women in general. Maybe he thought I was the bra thief. Who knew? But after pushing and tugging, gently as this was an antique, I got the thing in the apartment. I placed it in the front room. Definitely too pretty to be hidden in a bedroom no one sees, and currently no one does. I placed the drawers back in their slots and sat on my sofa admiring the most beautiful piece of furniture I've ever owned.

I had asked Jane to dinner, my treat, tonight and so I called her. She sounded funny on the phone. Fuzzy, as if I had just woken her from a nap.

"Can we delay this excursion for another night. The day was stressful and I'm not in a bright and cheery mood. Spare yourself the pleasure of my company. How about Saturday instead?"

"I'm afraid I'm busy Saturday night. Seeing Ian again. He rather grows on one. What can I say? I like him. As a friend that is, just as a friend."

"Then another time," said Jane. "Gotta go now." And she hung up. I was left staring at the phone in my hand. I don't remember a time when Jane had ever hung up on me.

My, my something's up with Jane. Best I drop in this weekend and get a handle on it. What was the mystery with her? Crap, another mystery... didn't I have enough.

Thursday dawned bright and clear. Damn, a rainy day would have given me an excuse to do nothing. I made a list:

1. Back to see the super and ask to see the registration form filled out by JOYCE

2. See what Martha found out about the visitors from Oklahoma

3. Another chat with Ginsberg

4. Find the dog-walking neighbor again. See if I can draw her out about what she saw, when, and the neighborhood in general

5. Find another neighbor, maybe canvas that whole street

6. Finally call Suzanne, Ian didn't say I shouldn't do so

I could see that my list contained references to both cases and was not in chronological or any specific order. That made for sloppy record keeping if nothing else. Not a good list.

I decided to switch tactics. Time to make a lovingly prepared, carefully edited report of expenses for dear old John and to stick it to him when I could by padding it sufficiently.

I took out another clean sheet of paper and titled it with no originality at all as 'Time Spent on the Case' so far.

Computer time four hours (at thirty dollars an hour)

Long distance phone call on my land line seven dollars and sixty cents

Interview time, including travel time, with the super plus the twenty-dollar bribe to get her to open up... one hour and forty-five minutes assuming I talked slow and drove even more slowly, make that two-hours

So far six hours times thirty dollars only amounted to one hundred and eighty dollars and twenty-seven-sixty in expenses... obviously I needed training in padding-the-bill. Since I'd already received one check for five hundred, I'd better come up with some way to justify it. Oh, and the seventy-five I owed Martha for the license plate info... I was now up to two-hundred and eighty-two sixty. Damn. Gotta keep tweeking. Obviously, I needed training in the fine art of creating an expense account or expensive accounting; whichever, I'd failed at both.

I had spent a lot more time and effort on Milton's case. Probably he was owing me now, despite the initial five hundred. I spent a half an hour writing down the interviews and times related to the Milton Smith inquiry. Paperwork, but necessary if I was ever gonna show a meaningful profit in this business of mine, much less pay for my new and beautiful chest. (Not the chest Milton was interested in obviously.)

I looked back at my list and decided to start with the call to Suzanne. I found the small piece of paper in my purse and punched in the number.

The phone was answered on the second ring.

"Suzanne Bournemouth here. Can I help you?"

I introduced myself. "Hi, Barbara Black here. I was hoping you could help me with some information about..."

Suzanne interrupted me. Her reply was short and to the point. I kind of admired her bluntness.

"This had better not be a sales call. Cause if it is you might just as well hang up now. You can't get blood from a turnip and, believe me, I don't even have vegetable juice."

Letting the strange mixed metaphor go, I said,

"No, this is Barbara Black. I've been hired to investigate the killing of your sister, Sarah Jane Smith, and I really would like to talk to you. I don't want anything from you but information. Knowing the victim, identifying with her often helps me to solve the case or at least put the final touches to what we believe is the possible guilt of J. Milton Smith..."

"Possible, my arse. That guy's guilty as hell. We don't marry well. Us Brisconce girls. We marry louses, creeps, but at least mine never tried to kill me. Tell you what, buy me lunch. Jenny's Diner. I'm a cheap date. In half an hour. It's on Speedway, south of Swan. You can find it and I'll spill my guts with everything I know about those two. But only if you buy. I'm running on fumes around here. Not that life was a lot better with my ex, Ian. He never made any money either. But I'm still job hunting. So, you buy. Okay?"

"Happily," I said. "See you there in thirty minutes." We hung up simultaneously.

Well, that was easy. She didn't ask for any ID or any anything. Or even query whose side I'm taking. I hope that lasts, but I'd better figure out what to say in case she does ask for proof of who I am and what right I have to the information about her sister. Maybe a barrage of questions from me will get her focusing on her answers instead of trying to figure out where I fit in. Let's see if that works. I felt momentary guilt about spending John's money on Milton's case, but only momentarily. Somehow it would all work out and how much could two hamburgers cost. Besides, right now, all my cash came from John Barker, my ex-husband with the deep pockets.

I hurried through a shower, donned jeans and a shirt and tennis shoes. Stuck the press pass made from an old newspaper billing into my pocket. (Well it had worked before hadn't it? Something about the newspaper title seemed to be as far into the document as some people read.) I also grabbed the letterhead with the attorney's name listed at the bottom of the long list of attorneys in the firm. Couldn't think of any other thing I had, well except my real PI license which was so recently dated it might not lend itself to great credibility. Still I rescued it from the top drawer of my desk and stuck it in my shoulder bag and headed out the door, checking for money and keys as I walked quickly toward the elevator.

And there he was, the neighborhood weirdo stepping into the elevator beside me.

"Hi," I said.

"Hi, back," he said.

That was it. I got off on the first floor and scooted out the door. He stood there watching me. Boy, we were making progress.

I glanced at my watch. Twenty minutes gone, ten to get there. Wonder if the sister resembles Sarah Jane or if I'll recognize her in some other fashion. How does mean and opinionated look?

nineteen

The diner was on a corner lot. It was fashioned of glaring aluminum siding to resemble diners everywhere. There were backless stools at a long counter. There was a lot of Formica and red faux leather upholstery in the area that held booths. Waitresses in red-striped garb stood around chatting with one another. Definitely not a busy day in the diner business. The room smelled in a good way mostly of bacon and French fries.

At the third table from the door a woman with long dark hair sat alone. Waiting for someone? Of slender build, she wore a long-sleeved white t-shirt, a pair of jeans and Sketchers. She looked neither to right or left, but stared straight ahead at the menu as I wandered up and asked, "Suzanne?"

She looked up revealing a thin face, and, underneath pale blue eyes, a small straight nose, an unsmiling rather prim pair of lips. She wasn't wearing any make-up that I could see. She nodded.

Well, I thought, a woman of few words though that was not my impression from our earlier phone conversation.

"Hi, I'm Barbara Black. Nice to meet you face-to-face." I sat down, took a laminated menu from the table. It was simple. Printed on both sides. No illustrations.

She looked up. Looked around for a waitress. Seeing none headed our way, she said.

"What do you want to know about my sister?"

"Everything, anything. Anything at all you care to tell me."

"Large perimeters, huh? Okay."

And she was off and running. She got off a dozen or more full and robust sentences, without taking a breath, before the waitress appeared at her elbow.

"Well, my sister was younger than me. We were the only two and we got along well most of the time. My parents were so enamored of one another that they didn't leave much room for Sally and me to breathe or be admired or attended to. Sally married early, that dolt of a husband of hers, in college. He and I, we never got along. I married much later than her. Oh, I was much more attractive than her, but took my time choosing. Had lots to choose from. Then I fell for an English chappie. Differences attract and we're as different as night and day. He's laid back and accommodating and I'm much more a person with my own agenda and beliefs. I don't tolerate slow very well and he's well, not mentally slow, but just slow moving, slow to make decisions, slow to pass judgements on people and situations. Too damn slow about everything to suit me."

She took a breath finally. What had I done? Uncovered another Ruth Ginsberg from the looks of things.

The waitress had made her way across the room to us. We placed our order. I simply ordered what she ordered hoping my debit card could stand the hit. After the waitress left, I asked,

"What makes you think Milton killed her?"

"Evidence. There's an eyewitness who saw him leaving so I've heard. And plenty of motive. My sister got on his nerves... a lot. She was quick witted, like me. She was quick to speak up too. Had stronger ideas than his. But she was also super-critical of everyone around her, including Milty baby. He wrote books. Not very good ones in my opinion and she collaborated on them with him. Edited, made suggestions, helped him with the plots. Otherwise, the rest of the time she was a little contemptuous of him. He was kinda slow moving and indecisive too. Didn't we marry a pair?"

"Would you have thought him to have a murderous disposition? That doesn't sound like something the man you described might do."

"What's that they say? "Revenge is a dish best served cold." Shakespeare, I think."

"Yes, something like that. But what I meant by my question was without the eye-witness and the other 'evidence' that you have heard, would you have thought Milton capable of murder?"

She paused a moment and then said, "Probably not. He's a little passive for that. Unless he was trapped. People do strange things when they're trapped."

I decided we'd had enough character analysis for one morning. Obviously, she wasn't fond of J. Milton or his type, but that wasn't going to get me anywhere.

"Did you know about Sally's affairs?"

"If you mean financial affairs, no. What do you mean?"

"I meant affairs of the heart, boy-friends, extra-marital affairs."

"Yeah, not who or where, but, yeah. I was just testing you, before I blurt out too much information. Don't want you judging the victim thinking she got what she deserved. I know she had something on the side. Ever since my divorce, I've been looking around too, keeping my eye out for Mr. Wonderful. But he hasn't magically appeared."

"Sorry to hear that. Mine either."

"Oh, you're in the sisterhood. Well, you're welcome to Ian but from my experience he is not nor could he become Mr. Wonderful."

Strange, I hadn't mentioned Ian to her. Had he mentioned me in one of their conversations. Perhaps that I might be calling. But she hadn't said so. I quickly decided to leave Ian out of our conversation as much as I could.

"Back to your sister."

"Nah, she never told me any names. She met these two guys, one, and then the other, in some fashion she never shared with me. Said they relieved the boredom and she didn't think Milton knew about them. Said they were okay. The second one was a good lover, better than the first but neither of them was worth ending her marriage. That's what she said about it."

"And you didn't ask?"

"No, basically I'm not a voyeur, I didn't want the dirty details."

She paused for a minute as if pondering her next statement.

"Now that I think about it, there was a guy named Bob and then the second one, he might have been Bill. Or have I got it backwards. I dunno. Wonder how she kept that straight. No last names though and the affairs were brief and physical and not particularly romantic. If there was a third, I didn't know about it. We didn't always talk that often."

Sarah Jane Brisconce Smith seemed to lack imagination when she picked her lovers, I thought. Bill and then Bob. What's with that? Real names or just keeping their identities to herself.

"And did she think Milton knew about her affairs?"

"No. She did not. She thought she'd gotten away with quite clever deceptions. That's what she thought. She coulda been wrong about that of course. But that's what she thought."

"What did she drive? There was a car still in the carport..."

"Yeah. That was hers. As a matter of fact, I did know something about her finances. She'd been saving up money for a new car for some time. She was planning on driving around town to various dealers with her old car, trying to make a deal on a new one. She favored Fords now. Heaven knows why. But she wanted something shiny and new, maybe a red car; she liked the Ford Focus. But something brand new or that at least looked brand new. She thought about answering ads too. People selling practically brand-new cars only and red ones and like I say that Ford Focus, she liked it. God knows why. Tin can in my experience, but she didn't think so and didn't care what I thought or anybody else's opinion for that matter, and she didn't even talk to Milton about it. Don't know how far she got in the process."

"So, did Bob or Bill sell cars?"

"I dunno. Coulda. She met the first guy about the time she got serious about getting a new car. Fire-engine red, she said. Sounds like she might have been looking for more than a car.

"At any rate, that's a possibility. She wouldn't meet anyone in the super-market as she and that husband of hers rarely cooked or ate together or anything. Though come to think of it, she did ask to borrow some of my cookbooks recently. When I got divorced, I didn't need them. Besides most of my recipes are here in my head. I didn't need the books."

I was learning more about Suzanne than I needed to know. More than I cared to know. So, she cooked. Perhaps Ian and I had better stick to eating out until I decided if I wanted any kind of relationship with him. Even as a friend, Ian might not stick around once he'd experienced my cooking.

"Back to the car thing. Do you know if she'd been actively looking and trying to trade in her old car or just driving around and glancing around? If you stop at any car sales venue, new or used sleezy or not, you get attention and you get someone showing you their wares."

"That's true. She wanted a good value for her old car. Thought it might have been a collector's item, but that I doubt. But yeah, I think she mighta been stopping at dealers and talking to salespeople."

"Do you remember what it was? The car she wanted to trade in."

"Oh, yeah. I'm not into cars much, but *she* liked 'em. Probably about twelve years old or more like fifteen, I'm not sure about that. It was a blue Chevy Impala. She'd kept it up real nice. She wasn't domestic. But she did keep that car spit and polished. Washed it often and spent some time turtle-waxing it. Whatever that is? Personally, I never saw a turtle that looked very shiny or clean."

"Neither have I. The wax may be made up of ground up turtle shells or something. Heck, I don't know."

"Well, you're the detective. You maybe should figure that stuff out."

"I wonder if I took the car around to the local Ford dealers. They might recognize it as one they almost got in trade. Do you think Bill or Bob was her first affair?"

"Well, I think it was Bill. She made some joke about Billy-Bob which combined both of their first names. Said she was going after a Bert next. No last names though. Or maybe a Charles. Maybe she said she'd spent enough time in the 'b's."

In the middle of our conversation the waitress brought milkshakes, fries and hamburgers. Apparently, the fare was not too simple for my new friend, though I'm not sure Ian's ex-wife enters the category of friend. But at this point who knows. Since John had taken all our old friends as his property, I was open to being friends with anyone. And another broke divorcee. What's not to like?

We chowed down in silence for a while. I could sit back and look at her. She wasn't an unattractive female. Not as cold and humorless as Ian had described her. People marry the wrong people almost as often as they marry the right ones. Maybe Ian and Suzanne weren't well suited. Her face had softened as we talked. She no longer seemed as wary of me as she had in the beginning. She lived alone. Hell, maybe she just needed someone, anyone to talk to and I was that lucky person. It helped. She'd given me some interesting details about Sally Smith.

I resumed my questioning.

"Anything else you can tell me. What kind of man did she find attractive?"

"Well, obviously not her own husband. He is short and well-built. Think he was a swimmer in college. So, she'd either go for tall or fat, the opposites you know. Maybe you're looking for a tall fat guy. Not something I'd rate as attractive. But my sister. She danced to her own tune. Who knows?" She took up her last fry between two slender fingers and popped it into her mouth. "Thanks for the burger and chips. I told you I was a cheap date."

Suzanne pushed her empty plate and glass away.

"Well, that does it for me. Thanks again. Look you hang on to my number and if you think of anything else you want to ask me, feel free to call. Next time we meet, it's my treat. Providing I can find two dimes to rub together."

She stood and walked out of the diner.

I sat for a moment. I might just call Milton Smith in the lock-up and see if I could borrow the Impala. Or maybe I'll just take a picture of it. Wouldn't need to call him for that. The less contact with Milton the better. So, I'll go with a picture. Time to visit some Ford dealers and see if anyone can remember that car and the woman who brought it in and better yet, the salesman she dealt with. Always a possibility. A slim lead is better than none at all.

The other thing I'd learned, Sally was already tired of affair number two, if she was looking for a change of alphabet. Maybe, just maybe she was ready to throw away simple affairs, or one-night stands or whatever, and maybe, just maybe, the man or at least one of them she was involved with was not willing to be so easily discarded.

twenty

I drove to the address in the Sam Hughes neighborhood and, with my phone in hand, entered the carport. Underneath a thin layer of dust was what appeared to be a 'ready to sparkle' blue car. Aha, the Impala.

I lacked a dust rag. No one about, I slipped off my t-shirt and was using it to dust the car when around the corner came a dog, sniffing about for something. Rather obviously I was a surprise to the dog. Not just being in my bra surprised him, but my very presence startled him so that he gave a sharp one-syllabled bark.

He looked familiar, shaggy creature that he was, and to my dismay I saw that he was on a leash. He was followed around the corner by a woman who looked familiar too. Was this the woman who discovered the body? I thought so.

"What are you doing here? Dressed or should I say undressed like that?"

I wasn't sure I owed her an explanation. It wasn't her property after all. But then what does constitute indecent exposure for a woman? I wasn't sure I wanted to risk that designation and didn't need her to call the cops, so I explained.

"I came to take a picture of the car. Didn't have anything to wipe the dust off with, so I used my top. Shocking, hmm? I didn't think anyone was around."

"Well, that was a rather foolish assumption, wasn't it?"

"I've got to agree with you there." I paused for a second and then added, "I think we've met. Not that previous acquaintance makes my appearance any more acceptable..."

"Yeah, we have met. You're that private investigator lady, aren't you? I thought you might have been a plain clothes kinda cop when we last met. Then I remembered you didn't show me no badge. I called the police and they didn't claim you. Said I didn't have to answer your questions if I didn't want to. But my curiosity got the best of me. I called the lawyer chap who was and is, I guess, representing John Milton Smith and he listened to my description and said who you was."

"Well, you're right. That's who I am. I'm a PI investigating Sally Smith's death. My purse is in my car. I have my license with me if you'd like to see it."

"Yeah, you go get it. But I think we've talked about all I know last time we met."

I pulled my now filthy t-shirt back over my head. That oughta take care of the risk of being accused of indecent exposure. I'd left my aging Toyota only a few steps out of the carport. I opened my car door as soon as I reached it. I grabbed my purse.

She loomed over my shoulder, her dog simultaneously sniffing my ankle. "You got a gun in there?"

I tried to straighten up to talk to her but was being crowded practically into a kneeling position by her and her mangy mutt. I slid sideways into the driver's seat and looked up at her.

"Could you make a little room for me to get out, please? And, no, I don't have a gun."

She shuffled back a few steps and pulled her dog with her. Really yanked him so the poor thing yelped. I was able to stand finally, and I opened my purse and pulled out the PI license. "See, I'm legit."

She took it from me and stared at it long enough to memorize its contents. "Now that you put your shirt back on, you look more like a bum. But I still can recognize you from the picture."

I stuck out my hand. "Barbara Black," I said.

"Lisa Manning." She took my hand and briefly, rather limply, shook it and then backed up a step or two more.

"Jacque and I were just having our walk. I swear I'm not coming near this house anymore. Dead bodies and half-naked women. It's just too much." She began to walk away, again tugging on the leash with little or no regard for the animal's comfort. He growled once. At her, I think, not at me. She loosened up a bit on the leash.

"You can see who picks our route, however. Damn dog. He's my husband's dog really, but I'm always cleaning up his messes. The dog and my man's as well."

Again, she started to walk away.

"Since we've run into one another again. May I ask a few questions or arrange with you for a more convenient time to do so?"

"Shoot... I wouldn't say that if you had a gun of course." She directed a hesitant smile my way indicating she was proud of her clever rejoinder.

The woman in front of me was a bottle blonde with a few black roots showing. She had a pleasant countenance. No great beauty, she was made-up carefully to look her best. She was well-rounded, chubby even, but not quite fat. Arizona-casual dressed, in a black, snuggly fitting, t-shirt, Levis and tennis shoes. Appropriate attire for walking a dog, even one you are not fond of. The Levis were a little too tight. That's all I noticed about her at the time. That and her grammar. Not too swift.

"So, Lisa Manning, how far from home does Jacque make you wander?"

"We live about three blocks that way. Nearer the University. My husband teaches there. At the U of A. He's a big deal professor."

"Did you walk by here every night?"

"Yep, still do. Jacque prefers this area to do his business. Dogs... who knows why."

"Was the night when you found Mrs. Smith's body the first occasion when you'd seen anything strange going on around this house?"

"Yep."

"Can you be sure the order of what you heard and saw that night?"

"Oh, Gawd, yes. First, I heard the shot, then I heard the car, a minivan, dark colored, and then the dumb animal pulled me over here and then we found her. Just like that. Just like I told the cops and you too and that attorney. That's all I got. I found her. I called it in. End of story."

"Did you see who was at the wheel of the minivan."

"No, but it was a man. I saw his outline. He had on a hat. It was a man's hat. Looked like one of those Bavarian let's-go-climb-a-damn-mountain kind of hats. I only got a glimpse as he was pulling out of the driveway, and then I got closer and found her. She was dead. Not moving and not breathing so far as I could tell. I sure wasn't gonna kneel down next to her and feel for a pulse or anything. There was some blood. Messy. I hate messy. The cops and the ambulance came right away, and they talked to me and then I went home. That's it. That's all I got."

Again, she took two long strides and began to walk away. The dog had gotten comfortable on a piece of grass near my car and awoke with a start as she pulled the leash taut where it was attached to the collar around his neck.

"Thanks," I yelled. "Could I get a phone number and address."

"No!" was what she yelled over her shoulder and then she was gone.

I used the camera on my phone to take a quick shot of the retreating forms of her and her dog.

I wandered back to the carport and took a quick couple of photos from the front of the Impala. Glanced around. Took off my top one more time and quickly dusted the side of the vehicle. Took another pic of the car from that angle and then donned my dirty t-shirt and headed home to the shower. I didn't look so much like someone who'd been photographing a car as like someone who'd been run over by one.

At home I looked her up. Lisa Manning was married to a Doctor of Science who taught Agricultural Economics at the U. His name was Timothy R. Manning, PhD. They lived almost four blocks from the house where Sally Smith died if my arithmetic and map skills were up to the task at hand. They had no children; paid their bills. Nothing remarkable about either of them that I could find. So, it wasn't as if she was rushing off home to be there for a child returning from school. She sure seemed in a hurry. Maybe she just was tired of answering questions. No one wants to find a body. That was thrust on her. I probably would get a little sick of the same questions over and over myself. I made a note of the address, phone number and husbands name and put it in my file. Time to print out the pictures of the car. I printed out the one of her and Jacque too and put it in the file along with copies of the pics of the car. I made more of those. Time to go visit some dealers in fine Ford Focusi, Forcuses just how would that word pluralize, anyway?

twenty-one

I reminded myself on the way to the first dealer that I needed to get back to figuring out who JOYCE is really and soon too. Thank god I only had two cases I was working on. Three would overwhelm me.

I had no success at the first Ford dealer I visited. I'd tried the direct approach with the picture of the Impala and a question about salesmen named either Bill or Bob and got nothing. Time to change tactics.

At the second one I found a quiet floor with nothing much happening and was literally rushed off my feet by not one but two bored salesmen. They had an eye contest with one another, and the winner hauled me away to his desk where a sign as well as a deep voice accompanied by a firm handshake announced that he was Roger Sawyers. The room was flooded with light from multiple shiny-clean floor to ceiling windows. Parked on the floor were gleaming autos in various colors and various sizes. Talk about glare! I hoped my make-up job could withstand that degree of light.

"So, you're interested in a new Ford, young lady. Nice choice on your part. We have a sale going on right now." He scowled slightly as he glanced out the door at my old car parked in full view of his desk and announced rather than asked, "That Toyota gonna be your trade-in. Looks like you're sure ready for a new car."

I took the opportunity while he was grimacing at my car to recover the picture of the Impala from my cell phone.

"No, actually I've just acquired this one and was thinking of trading it in. Or maybe not. Maybe the Toyota. I haven't quite decided." I placed the cell phone on the vast expanse of desk in front of him and touched the picture to lighten it up so he could view it easily.

"Well, the Impala would do you better."

"Probably it would."

He studied the photo a moment longer. "Say, I think that car was brought in here last month but by an entirely different lady. Older than you I guess, not so good to look at either, if you don't mind my saying so. Oh, don't get me wrong here. I'm not hitting on you. No, I get the Me Too Movement. But even a happily married man like me. I gotta admire beauty when I see it."

I managed a slight blush. Then I said, "Do you know what kind of offer was made on this car? It belonged to my Aunt Sally, but she just up and gave it to me. I'll bet you have a record of that offer. If you even know which salesman she dealt with?"

He turned on his computer and with his back to me typed on a few keys.

"Yeah, you're in luck. Bobby, he made her a pretty good offer. Would you believe $5,000 at trade and then it looks like the deal didn't go through. She was looking at a spankin new Ford Focus, last year's model though. The price has dropped a bit, you'd be glad to know. Course I'd have to have you bring in the Impala. But we can get started on the paper right now if you want to. Course maybe the Focus isn't what you want. We can go look around if you'd like."

Bingo. Bobby. Not Bill. This was apparently her most recent if I had the order of men friends correct.

"Is Bobby around? I'd like to meet him. Of course, the deal is yours, you understand. And yeah, the Focus is what I am interested in. A red one if you got it."

"Sadly, Bobby isn't here anymore. He moved to Denver to our dealer up there. Oh, two months ago now. So, no I can't introduce you."

"Well, she mentioned to me that she had met a salesman she liked. I just thought I'd say hello. Bobby..."

"Yeah, Bobby Andrews. Sorry you missed him, but we can work something out."

"Well, I'm not going to go to Denver, but if I do someday... maybe road tripping my new car... what is the dealership you're associated with there?"

This question I knew might be a little over the line, but so far Roger seemed to be enjoying our exchange. Maybe counting his commission put him in an affable mood.

"I only remember because it's such a stupid name. To me anyway. Jack Denver Ford in Denver, Colorado. How many people would think maybe this guy's ancestors founded the town. And they didn't."

I stood up. "Hey you're the best. A history lesson too. Why don't you give me your card, write the price of the new car on the back of it, taxes, fees, the 'out the door price' and if you can, the top price you can offer if the Impala meets your expectations. I'll take it to my tax accountant. He tells me what I can or can't spend. Then I'll be back."

He hesitated only a moment. Took a business card from the holder on his desk. Turned back to his computer. Tapped for a moment. In one swift moment he was out of his desk chair and had swiveled around to face some cubicles at the side of the large floor space. Gotta check with my manager he said. And before I could say anything at all he was moving away.

I checked out a game on my phone while he was gone and then put the phone back in my purse. When he came back, he was smiling. "This is what we can do for you, providing that Impala is in pristine condition..." And then he wrote some figures on the back of the card.

"You really should drive it before you go, Miss Shepard. I can get them to bring it around."

"I'd love to, but I'm on my lunch hour. Here, let me give you my information. With confidence I wrote Mary Jane Shepard and a phony phone number on the back of one of his other cards which I had plucked from the same holder.

"Just what is it you do, Miss Shepard."

I straightened up, slung my bag over my shoulder and smiled. "Oh, that's another very long story. Next time." I gave him my version of a disarming smile and headed for the door.

I will say this. Once again, he was quick on his feet and he managed to get around his desk and out of his cubicle and to reach the outside glass door before I did, so he could open it for me.

I knew he was watching closely as I headed out to my car. I Wondered how long it would take for him to find out that the person who drove in, in that car, was definitely not Miss Shepard.

I had found a Bobby person who was a car salesman. Probably could get a brochure from the Denver office to see if he was tall and fat, the victim's preferred body type. Maybe I'd found affair number one, and maybe not, but since the record of what they had offered was in the computer, then probably this was one of her men. But that's a lot of maybes. There were two more Ford Dealer's in town. This one was closest to her residence. Quite frankly, this didn't seem like a sure thing. And this Bobby, he was long gone out of town when Sally Smith was murdered. But he could have come back. Could have but probably didn't. I'm thinking probably not my guy. Nope. What next? I had some ideas, none of them promising.

twenty-two

I was feeling pretty discouraged when I got home. Checking my e-mail, I found the information from my friend Martha relating to the mysterious visitors to JOYCE or at least the car they arrived and left in. I let out a deep sigh as I opened the e-mail. I could use some luck.

Martha's e-mail gave me some more new names. The car was registered to a Jackson Barnes who was recorded to be twenty years old when he bought the car three years earlier. His address indicated, when I checked a map of the area around Oklahoma City, to be in a rural area maybe fifty miles from the outskirts of the city. My map showed postal codes, zip coded information that was usually reliable. I wondered if I should hire someone to look into this Jackson Barnes or maybe make the trip myself. A quick call to my ex should solve that problem.

I couldn't get in touch with John, but his secretary gave me permission to spend whatever I needed.

"Airline tickets don't worry John unless you're talking Europe. Tell me when and where and I'll book the flights for you, and arrange for a rental car at your destination."

So, I gave her tomorrow's date as the beginning and two days later the return trip. Strangely I didn't have to give her my reasoning or even information about my mission.

Apparently, saying that my trip was necessary to the "research" I am doing for John was all the information Lucy, his gal Friday, needed. My assumption is that John is doing really well. I had to wonder what kind of fool I was to give up the easy life which apparently had become even easier than I ever imagined.

Lucy also said, "Just give me some info on your debit card and I'll fund it with some expense money right now."

I complied within seconds.

Lucy said,

"I'll put in a thousand. Save your receipts though. Call me when you get back and you can report on what you've learned to John if he's around then. Right now, he and the Princess are out of town. Won't tell you where. I don't want to rub your nose in it."

"Thanks."

That was all I could think to say. Apparently, Lucy knew what there was to know about my former relationship to her boss. Probably thought I was some kind of idiot to give all that up. The sarcasm implied in the 'Princess' title hinted she might not totally be enamored of JOYCE either. Well that made two of us.

I called my cousin Jane when I got in. Gave her the information about my trip. She didn't show a lot of interest. Definitely needed to talk to her when I get back. What is happening with Jane? Not only am I getting the cool shoulder from her but, all of a sudden, she seems a little secretive. Maybe my seeing Ian bothered her. She thought he was too old for me. I'd never noticed her getting upset about my not taking her advice before now. Whatever had pissed her off, it was mild. She wasn't hanging up on me or anything like that. She just seemed self-absorbed and for cousin Jane, that was a new aspect. One I didn't remember encountering ever before in her rather straightforward, right to the point way of communicating with me.

I called my new friend Ian and left a message on his answering machine. Maybe I didn't owe him any explanation. But we had a sort of second date in the offing, actually more than sort of. It was planned for this Saturday night and I'd be gone. I asked for a rain check in my message saying I'd be out of town. I liked Ian. I did not want to lose that connection. I'm not happy when I'm living like a total isolate and right now that seemed to be my path.

I began my packing for the next day. The bad thing about packing a suitcase is that once you've laid your stuff out on the bed it becomes one of those mindless activities. Fold and tuck are not things that occupy your mind. I began thinking about my relationships. Wasn't like the list was long and as far as I knew things were good with Ian. So, my thoughts turned to cousin Jane. We had been so close and then Ian came along.

All of us, women for sure and men maybe, have experienced that sensation. You've got a 'bestie 'and she meets Mr. Right or you do. Soon phone calls aren't returned, and coffee dates are broken. You've run into a distracted and absent best friend who ignores you. This is the side of this woman, or girl (it begins early) you had never seen before. It goes back to Junior High if not to cave women. I've been both victim and perpetrator. In those old days I remembered we had techniques to cope with the disappearance of a best friend from your day to day life and the subsequent blow to one's ego.

One could wait until the infatuation faded, be around for the tears and the reassuring hugs. Another way of coping was to form a new clique of friends and exclude in turn one's former 'bestie'. Hollow victories all. And not appropriate solutions for my present predicament with Jane. I like to tell myself I'm way past junior high and its methods.

I tucked the last pair of trouser socks into the suitcase and made a decision. I'd just go see Jane and find out. I'd ask her. "What the hell is the matter with you?" seemed a little strong. I'd think of a better opening gambit as I drove.

The drive was swift except for the quick stop-off at McDonalds to purchase a chocolate milkshake. There is not much in this world that chocolate won't solve. The combination of ice-cream and chocolate is the universal cure for whatever ails you.

As I drove around the corner toward the entrance of Jane's apartment complex, I witnessed a puzzling phenomenon. Across the way on the same side of the street at the front door of the three-story building where Jane resides, I saw my John (well actually JOYCE's John if one wanted to stay current and accurate) climbing into his car. He didn't see me. I pulled to the curb and sat there. Jane and John and JOYCE and me... not even a clever triangle but definitely an awkward square. John didn't even like Jane. Or he hadn't liked her in the very recent past. He'd called her one of my 'loser' relatives as I recall. And too, he was also out of town according to Loyal Lucy, his secretary, unless she was lying for him or maybe John had a doppelganger. And in all fairness, maybe he had never gone. John is quixotic and often changes his mind and his travel plans.

What the hell is going on, I asked myself, not Jane, and having no potential for an answer I slipped the car into drive, pulled out into the street and drove home, fuming all the way.

twenty-three

I spent a restless evening always the case for me and air travel and doubly aggravated now by my morbid curiosity about the John/Jane connection. Romance? Friendship? Friends with privileges? I had no idea. I tried to nap and had no luck. Sleep even in its most abbreviated form wasn't going to visit.

My flight left at midnight. I decided to leave my car at the airport. Lucy had arranged a direct flight for me to Oklahoma City. And she put me in first class, which I did appreciate. After all expenses were on John, that rat, and I would soak it to him any way I could.

From the airport I took a shuttle to the closest hotel and slept a while, getting up a little after eight finally, and helping myself to the hotel breakfast buffet. Keeping in mind that I was only a few pounds away from curvy becoming hefty, I ate sparingly.

By ten-twenty local time, I was back at Terminal One to find the car rental agency. I approached AVIS and got myself a mid-sized rental, a Ford Focus for old time's sake; just last week I had claimed the desire to own one. It came equipped with a nav system. I plugged in the address of the home either owned or rented by Jackson Barnes and was on my way. I rolled down the driver side window and soon breathed clean country air as I headed south towards Ardmore.

At some point as I neared my destination, I stopped the questions in my mind that raced around continually trying to tie my ex-husband to cousin Jane. I began to think of how I was going to handle the situation when I found Jackson Barnes and maybe his younger sister. If that was the relationship the two shared. And, then, what relationship did they both share with JOYCE? I had plenty of questions and not a clue as to where the answers might take me.

When I neared the rural route the identity of which I had so carefully written down, I was well into the countryside. After I passed the minimal town center, the wood-frame house appeared. Clearly visible from the highway, the house wasn't much more than a shack. A dusty, narrow track led to the house. An old beat-up truck sat forlornly in the yard. There appeared to have been no attempt towards planting either a garden or trees in the scruffy yard. The whole property reeked of a dismal degree of neglect.

I turned around and headed back to the buildings that sat at the crossroads. I was doubtful they would qualify as a town. A run-down gas station appeared at the intersection's eastern border. Two rusty pumps stood like lone sentries marking the entrance to the town. Next to it, a metal sign above the peeling-painted exterior walls of the bar and grill would appear to have once upon a time said 'SMITTY'S', but the S was missing. It simply read MITTY'S. Maybe there was really a Mitty around somewhere, but I doubted it.

Across the street sat a small general store. Two sales posters placed at odd angles from one another decorated the grimy window. The posters looked like giant eyes gazing sadly out on the time-worn rural buildings. A little further down the road I saw what appeared to be a grade school, even though no sign indicated its purpose. There were children out on the small dusty playground kicking a ball around and they looked to be somewhere between six and nine years of age; hence a grade school. I decided to do some shopping in the small general store. See what I could pick up about the Barnes family farm and its occupants.

As I entered the store there was the jingle of a bell to announce my arrival. A dowdy woman, wearing a faded housedress and old lady shoes, those black things with fat heels and laces, stepped out of a back room and stood behind the counter. I walked down the central isle of the store. Looking up, she spoke to me.

"Anything I can help you with, Honey?"

I'd invented my cover story hastily as I walked across the street. I stuck out my hand toward the woman and said,

"I'm Mary Martin from Los Angeles. I'm in your charming town on a mission. Driving through it, I saw, oh, at about another two miles out of town, a little house, perfect for my purposes anyway. It's on the left side of the road."

The woman nodded and folded her arms, the fat on her upper arms jiggling as she moved. She ignored the hand I had left sticking out in front of me. I let my hand drop.

"I'm scouting for a place to film parts of the movie, *Look Homeward Angel* and, boy, does the town look just like the one depicted in the book. And that little house with the weathered siding is just about perfect."

The woman gave me a blank stare. "That's a thing I've never heard of about this town or its houses, but if you say so..."

"What can you tell me about the owner? We pay well, but sometimes we need to rent the location for a couple of months and have the owner move out while we film. Is this owner or the family, are they easy to talk to? Can I just go over there now, do you think?"

"Yeah, well he goes by the name of Jackson, Jackson Barnes, and he's a little bit weird even for this little ole town. Sticks to himself. Doesn't talk to me when he comes in here. Spends some nights drinking beer at Smitty's, least I hear tell he does. Not too sociable over there, but he's made some pals with a few of the men 'cause he no longer sits by hisself all the time."

She took a breath and plunged on. I let her talk.

"His sister used to live with him. Moved up to Oklahoma City when she finished up at the high school. Hasn't been back to see him since to my knowing. Had an older sister who was married to the old man. Jason Smith was his name, lots of Smiths around these parts. He lived in that little house, farmed a bit and then married this young pretty gal who moved in with him and brought her young brother and sis with her. They was there about four years and then the old man moved to Florida, took her with him. Left the kids there. Haven't seen hide nor hair of either of them two since."

"Sounds like he could use the money and the break from his place. I'll go on by and talk to him."

"Okay by me ifn you do. This town could use the excitement of a filmin' crew. S'pose they might shop here. That'd be all right with me."

That was as much of an endorsement as I was going to get. The screen door slammed behind me and chimed again as I left.

As I drove out of town, I spied the old pick-up truck I had seen sitting in the yard at the little house. It was parked outside of the Smitty's of the missing S. Since it hadn't been there five minutes ago, I supposed I might have a chance to check out the house before I made any attempt to meet Jackson Barnes.

I drove swiftly down the small, narrow blacktop. Full of potholes, it shook my small car as if a large arm had picked it up and tossed it around. There was barely enough room for two sedans to pass one another. I looked over my shoulder to judge whether I could be seen leaving the roadway. The town was too far away, for my actions to be observed. There was no passing traffic, and no one behind me either. I decided to pull into the track and take a quick look around.

The story of the old man and the young bride with the two younger siblings was intriguing. If the older woman, but not much older than her siblings, had been the bride of the old farmer might that woman have been JOYCE? And JOYCE hadn't ended up in Florida. I should have asked more about the names, but then what would a site locator want that info for? If JOYCE hadn't ended up in Florida, then had the old man really gone there? If not, where was he now?

The house was even less impressive when I got closer. I got out of my car and listened for the growl or bark of a dog and saw or heard none, yet there were little piles of dog turds in what would have been the lawn if any grass had been nurtured there.

I entered the unlatched screen door onto the porch. The porch was narrow and empty of anything but a pair of old boots and a year's supply of dust and dirt. The door into the house sat ajar. My curiosity got the better of me. I couldn't remember a time when people didn't lock up in Tucson or any place I've ever lived. I decided to take a quick peek. I justified my action thinking Jackson left the door open for me on purpose and my license said private investigator so surely that is what a proper investigator would do. Even I didn't find that argument believable.

The door on the house creaked a little as I opened it further. Still no pets. I was greeted by air reeking of stale cigarette smoke. I stepped inside and encountered what I assume was a living room. A few feeble rays of the mid-day sun lit the interior. I didn't see any light switches. It was still early enough that I could make out most of the furnishings in the dimly lit room. There was a coffee table, marred with cigarette burns and, on its surface, two identical overflowing ashtrays. No family pictures about in frames. On the floor beneath the coffee table, I found what I was looking for. An old fashioned red faux-leather album sat gathering more dust, its pages held in place by a dull red cord.

I picked the album up. Blew off the dust. Opened it up to a picture of JOYCE, a younger man and a much younger girl and, standing behind them all was a grim looking forty-five to fifty-five-year-old man. I pulled the picture out to look at it more closely. As I held it up close to my face, I heard the sound of a truck approaching the house.

My first instinct was to run. So I followed it. I dropped the album on the coffee table keeping the picture for myself and sliding it into my pocket. I upset one of the ashtrays in the process so that the ashes, the book and some of the cigarette butts went sliding off the table onto the floor. I moved toward the door. So much for leaving no trace of my presence inside the house. I reached the door, jerked it open, flew onto the back porch and then stilling myself and taking a deep breath I walked, at what I hoped to be a leisurely pace, out of the screen door onto the steps, once again pulling the door tightly closed behind me.

The man, not so young as he had been in the purloined photograph, and looming much larger in real life, had just stepped out of his truck. A dog, the obvious source of the piles of turds in the yard, leapt out of the bed of the pick-up truck and headed straight toward me. Neither of them was smiling.

"Blue! Drop It, Blue!"

I assumed the 'it' was meant to refer to me. Though in a matter of inches he would reach me, the creature's jowls had not yet closed on my arm. At the sound of the command the dog dropped to his stomach. He lay still watching me. Not once did his eyes leave my face. Still, I felt a sense of immediate relief that at least for the moment he was not going to have to actually drop 'it.' I decided, wisely, not to move.

"What the hell were you doing in my house, Lady?"

Too nervous to re-invent, I said. "I'm scouting for a place to shoot a motion picture. Your house seemed perfect. Most of our interior shots are done on stage sets in Hollywood but occasionally the director likes some exterior shots that show someone entering the house. I was just looking..."

The dog was still laying there in the dirt, but his ears pointed forward. Still afraid to move, I risked sticking my hand out a short distance from my body in a 'willingness to shake' manner. "Mary Mattingly," I said, thinking the Mary Martin reference might not go over with this guy. "We rent houses to make movies, sometimes for months on end for a pretty good price I might add. In the five figures. You might have to move out for a time, but we make it worth your while to do so."

Two pairs of eyes still studied me unwaveringly. But one pair warmed up slightly. The man's face broke into a grin. "Let's go talk this over. Come on inside."

"If you... if you... would get that dog away somewhere, I'd be happy to talk to you... Let me get my check book out of the car first."

"Ole Blue make you nervous, does he? Well, that's his job. Sure lady, I'm gonna lock him into the bedroom, then you come on in and we'll talk the details, where, when and how much."

The man, Jackson Barnes, walked toward his house. He signaled with a snap of his finger for Blue to follow him. The dog gave me one more penetrating look then followed his master somewhat reluctantly onto the porch. The screen door slammed shut behind them.

I'm the first to admit I am not long on courage. Digging into my purse for the keys which miraculously just this once were on top of the heap of the other miscellany that made up its contents, I made a mad dash for my car. Jumped in, stuck the key in the ignition and, as soon as the motor turned over, jammed my foot on the gas, wheeled in a wide circle around the red truck and drove back down the rutted track.

As I reached the highway, I saw in my rear-view mirror, Barnes, unaccompanied by Blue, rushing towards his truck to follow me. As I emerged onto the pavement, I made a decision that may well have been the wrong choice. I headed back to town. That way led to people and eventually to Oklahoma City. The other direction, I had no idea. On these roads, with Barnes in hot pursuit going off into what was the unknown territory could lead to a situation which had 'advantage Jackson Barnes' written all over it.

I fled down the highway with Barnes in pursuit. Hoping to have at least one witness to whatever lay ahead, I pulled into the parking lot of the general store That's when my luck ran out.

I dropped the damn keys on the floorboard of the car. I lost a valuable minute as I fumbled on the floor for them. Picking the keys up I lost another thirty seconds searching for the handle on the unfamiliar auto. As I got out of the car, I turned to lock it. Thrusting the keys deep into my pocket, I heard the roar of Barnes truck pulling into the parking lot. He was not yet in my sight or fortunately me in his. Unwisely I had pulled snuggly up to the side of the building. Seconds later, Jackson Barnes pulled in behind me succeeding in blocking me, cutting me off from any hope of a quick and easy departure.

I dropped back inside the rental car. As I rolled down my window, he was out of his truck and just as quickly in my face.

"What the hell were you doing in my house. In my business. Looking at my photo album. Just who are you anyway and what do you want?"

I tried to sound patient and not frightened though I knew my knees were wobbling.

"I told you. And then when I got to the car, my checkbook wasn't in my purse. I don't like your dog and I wasn't going to risk going back to your house and meeting up with Ole Blue again, so I drove back to town."

It didn't convince me, so I doubted if my statement would convince him. And as it turned out...

"I don't believe a damn word you're saying. I'm getting the sheriff, and I'll just leave my truck right where it is now. You ain't going anywhere this time, lady, and you better believe it. I'm gonna go get Sheriff Joe. He's gonna want to talk to you about breakin' and entering."

He stomped away, and then as an afterthought turned and said to me, "You wait right here. I'll be back before you know it." Nothing like stating my fears for me.

twenty-four

I considered my options. Few to none. I opened the car door and was quickly standing upright outside the car. I leaned back inside and took my wallet out of my purse. Took my PI license as well and my cell phone. I quickly turned the phone onto silent mode. Closed the purse, thought about its contents and chose not to lock the car door. I slid the key to the car back into my pocket. I took a quick look around and seeing no one, lay down in the crab grass and slid not too graciously under the car.

In my defense it was the only option I could think of. The clerk in the grocery store could be turned into another ally of Barnes. Probably these locals would stick together against an outsider. If the sheriff was Barnes' pal all the locals might well side with the sheriff if not with Jackson Barnes himself.

Another car pulled into the parking lot. A door slammed. I heard voices but couldn't make out what they were saying. Barnes and someone wearing official looking boots and a stripe on his pants walked up to my car.

"Well, she ain't here now."

Answered by Jackson Barnes' unmistakable twang. "Well, she'll be back now, won't she? She ain't goin nowhere without this car."

He opened the car door. "Look, she left her handbag here."

"Leave it," said the second voice. "We'll make her open it when she gets here. That's the legal way and we'd better keep it legal. At least till we figure this out. Come on. We can watch from Smitty's. The window in the back booth looks right out on this spot."

The boots and voices moved away. I heard a door slam across the street. Now or never I thought, squirming my way out from under my rental car. Once free of the car I ran in a crouch to the opposite side of the parking lot and into a dense copse of trees. Catching my breath, I looked up just as a Greyhound bus pulled into the lot. Barely missing the combination of my car and Jackson's truck, the bus pulled in tightly behind it.

The door of the bus slid open and three passengers got off followed by the bus driver, a portly man wearing at least part of a driver's uniform, the cap and the trousers. He pulled on the jacket as he followed his passengers into the store.

The Greyhound was parked just west of Jackson's truck allowing me to slip around the end of the huge bus and quickly make my way to the door. The bus driver had apparently latched the door closed. I stood exposed for anyone to see when he or she left the country store. Fortunately for me, the bus driver came out first, carrying a sweating Pepsi bottle in his right hand. He strolled across the lot toward me.

"Can I help you, young lady?"

By some alchemy I failed to observe, he caused the bus doors to open.

"Are you heading toward Oklahoma City?" I asked.

"Yep, you need a ticket. You'll have to get it inside," and he gestured with his left hand toward the store.

"Can I talk to you about that... inside? I opened my wallet just enough so that he could glimpse my lump of cash which looked rather impressive though it mostly contained ones and not twenties.

He stepped inside. I followed quickly, gratefully sinking into the front seat just opposite where the driver now sat. I hoped my presence in the bus, viewed from the other side of the street, was blocked by the high back of the driver's chair.

"Here's the deal. I don't want anyone to know I'm leaving. It's a domestic matter. My husband is trying his damnedest to keep me here and the sheriff is his best buddy. I'd like to pay you cash to get me out of town." I drew out the equivalent of two-hundred dollars in twenties leaving my wallet empty of all but some ones, and handed the bills to him.

"If I give you this. Can you hide me, cause the sheriff might come lookin'. I can get you one hundred more when we reach Ardmore, or, Oklahoma City if you're going that far. Just need an ATM..."

"You got yourself a deal, little lady, but we gotta move fast. My passengers will be back soon."

He moved quickly, for such a stout fellow, to the back of the bus. I scurried along behind ducking as low as I could, thankful that many of the passengers had pulled the shades down on their windows. When we got to the back, he opened a tall, narrow door. "

"Excuse the smell, but this is where I store my dirty laundry. And you're going to have to stand up and hug this stuff to you to keep it from falling out. You can change buses in Ardmore. I'll settle for just one hundred more. Ardmore's only about an hour's drive. You'll be all right. Now get in there and pull this stuff around you in case that husband of yours decides to search."

As he talked, he pulled the clothing off the pile on the floor and handed it back to me. I climbed into the back of the compartment. He bent over and tucked a big shirt around my legs. He placed a dingy undershirt snuggly around my face. The door closed just as I heard voices, and not too many minutes later I heard the reassuring sound of the engine starting up.

Before we could get into motion, I heard a banging on the door of the bus and then a too familiar voice sounded,

"Hey Benjamin, how you doin', man?"

A second less familiar voice sounded before Benjamin, the bus driver, could respond to the first question.

"How many passengers you got?"

The driver's voice responded firmly, without so much as a quaver. "Three."

"Any of them join you here?"

"Nope, this bunch has all been with me since well before the Texas border."

I could only guess how far down the aisle Jackson was when I heard his voice way too close to my hiding place.

"Yep, three passengers just like the man said and not a pretty young woman among them." Then he added, "Excuse me for saying so, Mam, as I could tell you was pretty fine looking when you were younger. Just this gal we're lookin' for is young, and you, not so much anymore."

I didn't know whether he had improved his case with the female in question or not. For his sake I hoped she was a really old lady, or he might find his eyes clawed out.

A minute later I heard, "See you around, Bennie."

I heard the door close and felt the bus lurch forward. I held on to the sides of my closet not wanting to fall out onto the floor of the bus. Exposure was the last thing I needed with the likelihood that Jackson Barnes and the sheriff were standing just outside and watching as the bus was driven away.

twenty-five

It's a fairly short story from here. I managed not to pass out from the fumes emanating from the man's underwear. Couldn't help but wish he showered a little more often.

In Ardmore, he let me out of the closet after the last passenger left. I had managed to maneuver around to get the last hundred I had promised him out of a travel wallet I carried suspended from my bra and tucked into my pants. He graciously accepted it without a word and showed me the door of the depot. Once inside I bought a ticket with my credit card and settled down to wait for the Oklahoma City bus. Not quite a half an hour later I was on my way. On the trip I decided that once back in Arizona, I would mail the key back to the rental agency in the Oklahoma City Airport and have them pick up the car. It had GPS. They would find it and the hefty fine would get paid by my ex."

When I got to the Oklahoma City airport, I had second thoughts. It might be just like John to reject the fee. I made my way over to the rental agency.

There was a middle-aged male with pale blue eyes and a weak chin on the desk. My ideal type for the purpose. I thrust the key at him.

"Your damn car broke down on me in the middle of Nowhere, Oklahoma. You find it. You got GPS, don't you? You bring it back. I got to get on to Tennessee right now. Next time check out your car first so that when it overheats it will still start again, or, better yet, fix it so it doesn't overheat. Now I got a deadline, I gotta go."

The clerk was left standing there, mouth agape, staring at the key as I walked back to the terminal just in time for them to call my flight. The best defense is a good offense or so they say. There might still be a whopping big fine, but I had a fighting chance of them buying my story this way. Thankfully, he had not glanced down at his paperwork to see that my destination was really Tucson. The last thing I needed was to have him send someone to find me in the Delta departure lounge. I was almost as grateful when my flight was called early as I had been when the driver had closed the bus door after the visit from the sheriff and Jackson. This time, however, I could breathe my sigh of relief out loud.

I planned to send the car rental agency an email when I got home, telling them, not asking them, for my purse and my suitcase to be sent to Tucson ASAP. We'd see where that went, most likely into the trash. I reviewed the value of the clothing in my case, and the stuff in my purse and realized I could live quite nicely without any of it.

When I formulated my report for John, I would hint that the reason the man, Jackson Barnes, had been so secretive might have to do with the disappearance of Jason Smith and of his wife, aka JOYCE, wife of John-my-ex. Where had Jason Smith gone? Later, I was able to check out databases in Florida and starting in the year Jason Smith had disappeared from Oklahoma I was not able to find any new Jason Smith's appearing in Florida's phone records anywhere. Wonder what JOYCE would say about all this?

My other question would be asked first of Jane. What was she doing with my ex? That's what I wanted to know.

I arrived back in Tucson and stumbled from the plane to the exit. On my way to the parking lot I realized that leaving my luggage in the lurch had actually worked out. No standing in kiosk lines to retrieve my baggage. No baggage. Whee! Perhaps that is what freedom is all about. And then I began to wonder what kind of immediate future awaited me. My choices seemed to be a midnight run on a self-serve laundromat, or, a trip into the dark recesses of the laundry facility in my scary basement. I asked myself that proverbial all-important question. What did I own that was clean and awaiting my return? I wanted to stand in a hot shower, wash the weariness away and go about my business on the morrow in some state other than complete and stark nakedness.

I found my car. Paid at the exit with my credit card, receiving a frown from the night attendant.

Maybe she preferred cash. Maybe she preferred being left the hell alone. The happiness or lack thereof of the parking lot attendant was not, nor should it be, a major concern of mine.

I tried to think about the case, about JOYCE and my ex on the way home from the airport, but quite frankly I no longer had any ideas. Except to be as sure as I could be that JOYCE had not shared her total history with John. And, did it really matter? Had he moved quickly on to my cousin Jane. Rude of him if he had. First of all, it indicates he can't stay faithful to anyone and secondly, dammit, Jane was all I got in the divorce decree. He took the rest of the friends and relations. Couldn't he just leave Jane for me?

I found a parking place on the street quite nicely aligned with the entrance to my building.

The lock accepted my key and the doorknob turned in my hand. Happily I entered a quiet relatively orderly space that was mine, all mine.

Hanging in the closet I found two blouses to choose from and one pair of slacks. In my chest of drawers plenty of panties and one bra that was really just a titty cover, no uplift, no nothin, but it would do. A quick shower, an old nightgown found in a bottom drawer and I crashed. No thought for how I would pursue anything the following day. Tonight, I was bent on pursuing snow-white sheep as they leapt over a low barrier in perfect alignment with one another.

I didn't even set an alarm. I didn't even check my messages. I sought oblivion and that is what I found.

My eyes opened wide at seven in the morning, and closed again quickly. Hours later, when I finally awoke, it was to the insistent ringing of the phone, which ceased as soon as I reached a hand toward it. Time for coffee, ugh. I remembered I don't like coffee. So, time for orange juice, none, Pepsi, none, okay, time for instant tea. I threw a slice of bread in the toaster. It already stood upright on its own; I was pretty sure toasting wasn't going to do much for it. Lacking butter, I swathed the toast in a blob of peanut butter, thinking surely peanut butter is kissing kin to butter even though cows had nothing to do with the latter. I took a bite. Not bad enough to make me gag. Therefore, acceptable. Carrying glass and toast, I made my way to my small living room to eat, relax, and think.

Nothing. No ideas.

Back in the kitchen I turned on the answering machine. There were five messages but for the life of me I could not remember how many I had left on the machine. Still it was flashing its little neon light at me, a sure indicator that at least one of them was recent.

Two of the messages were from Ian. A thinking of you, wondering what you're doing sort of theme emerged. Nothing urgent. A curt, "call me" message from John, nothing new in that tone of voice either. A question from his secretary, Lucy, "Say, Barb do you know anything about a rental car that didn't get returned to AVIS in Oklahoma City?" The final message was from my cousin Jane. I decided to return that one first.

When I called her apartment, I got no response. It was a weekday, so I assumed she was at her job. I left a message requesting she give me a call.

I called John's secretary next. Lucy answered on what I presumed was her private line.

"Hey, Lucy, good morning."

She apparently recognized my voice. "So, Barb, welcome home. I assume you have returned to the Old Pueblo."

"Correct," I said. "Late last night or I would have called you. Yeah, I left a car stranded near Ardmore, Oklahoma. Damn thing wouldn't start, and I was in an uncomfortable situation so didn't want to lean on the locals for help. Took a bus back to Oklahoma City and gave the key of the unreliable vehicle to the car rental agency. They said they'd get it back and check it out. What did you hear from them? I guessed they would call you since you arranged it for me and listed John's firm as my employer on the form."

"Well, a couple of things. One, they said it started like a charm. Was found outside a general store in this tiny little no name town. No one approached them so they got in it and drove away. They think we owe them for the inconvenience of picking it up. The fee is a mere two-hundred dollars, but they are demanding we pay it. And I can't see anything in their typical contract that excuses us from returning it to the place it was rented from. How do you feel about that?"

"I say pay it. Maybe I flooded it. I dunno, I was anxious to leave because I felt very vulnerable sitting there in the middle of nowheresville with the sheriff and his buddy, a brother, I believe, of John's very own wife, our ever-lovin' JOYCE... well I'll explain it all to him. But pay it. The sooner I put that incident behind me the better I'll feel."

Lucy said, "Okay, at your request I'll pay it. But you'll need to explain it to John. He'd like to see you since you're back. Today or tonight. You name the when and where, he told me. But today or tonight."

"Okay, Lucy. Tonight, it is. Not until nine p.m. and he can name the where. If that doesn't work for him then the best I can do is tomorrow."

"I'll get back to you." And the line went dead.

twenty-six

I tried a call to Jane's school, leaving a message for her to call me if possible as soon as her workday was over. That left me free to unpack. Free to call Ian, maybe... maybe I'd wait a day. I did want to talk to the young attorney. See if anything on J. Milton Smith had turned up since I was out of town. I left a message for him too. Then went into the bedroom to unpack and found of course that unpacking was out of the question. My suitcase still sat in Oklahoma. Should have asked for word of it from Lucy. When in doubt check my finances on-line. There was, for a change, plenty of money. John had deposited two checks plus my severance pay. Time for shopping.

At the grocery store I bought orange juice, Pepsi, bananas, and bread. A full shopping as far as I was concerned. I made a side trip to Kohls. A little underwear, a shirt, a pair of jeans and some really cute sandals, and I was home again in half an hour.

Then I sat by the phone for a full forty-five minutes, waiting for someone to return my phone calls. I ate a banana, lunch. Had a glass of orange juice, snack. And waited some more. I started to write some notes about Oklahoma, but in retrospect the whole adventure didn't make much sense. I decided that telling it in sequence would be the best bet.

Lucy called with a report that my suitcase and purse were on the way. Fed Ex, collect. The two hundred had mollified the rental agency. John said nine p.m. was too late. He would buy me breakfast tomorrow at seven a.m. at the Bisbee Breakfast Club on Wilmot Road. Bring my report."

Lucy hung up.

Ten minutes later Ian called. I told him I was expecting work related calls and would give him a call this evening. He agreed though he did sound a little hurt. Ah, well, friends and relations and business would all hold. I told my little rebellious self, my curiosity about Jane and John must be satisfied. I WANNA TALK TO JANE NOW....!!!**##!!

The phone rang one more time. It was the youthful attorney of J. Milton Smith.

Without preamble he introduced himself and then asked. "Where you been? I've been wanting to talk to you."

I gave him a limited explanation. "I've been out of town on another case. Do we know anything more about Milton Smith's situation? Have you been able to arrange bail?"

"No and no," the man of few words replied.

"The District Attorney sees him as a possible flight risk. Plus, he has no money other than what he paid you. And no, nothing new. You're the one who's supposed to bring in some new ideas. Call me when you know something." And he hung up.

Finally, Jane called.

I asked, "Have you got some time to have dinner with me? We need to have a chat."

"Fine."

"I'll pick you up in fifteen at your apartment, if that's okay. We'll go for dinner. My treat."

"Fine. But make it forty-five. Good God, Barb it's only 4:30. Let's leave the early dining to the old folks, okay?"

"Fine, an hour then. See you."

I put on my new shirt and Levis and really cute sandals. The cuteness had quadrupled since I brought them home. I wondered when my suitcase would arrive. Just as I was wondering the Fed Ex people called to tell me my package would arrive tomorrow from one to three and that I owed them sixty-seven dollars for shipping costs. Okay then. I'd simply charge it to John.

Since I had time to kill, I got out an accounting pad and began to prepare the bill of my expenses for John. Not that I didn't have them covered by the deposit to my charge card, but I felt I ought to itemize the monies I had spent on my trek to Oklahoma and the charges that had followed me home as well.

Airline tickets – oops no, Lucy had purchased those

Hotel room

Car rental and additional fees

Bus tickets inclusive of the bribe I had paid the driver to sneak me out of town.

Lost luggage return fees

Meals and beverages

I thought the few drinks on the plane home from Oklahoma were well deserved for the trauma of my day and the narrow escape from angry natives. There, that should cover it. I was ready for John tomorrow in the a.m. Then there was my hourly fee. I'd been gone nearly thirty-six hours. He could just pay me a nice round figure for my time.

I picked myself up off the couch and headed for the door.

twenty-seven

As I neared Jane's apartment. I could not help but wonder if I'd see John there again. I'd settled on a meal with Jane at a quiet older restaurant where we could have a drink. I thought the drive across town might be helpful too. Maybe we could talk better if our eyes weren't on one another. If she needed to lie to me, and she might, lying is a lot easier if you're not making eye contact while you're doing it. At least that is my experience.

I was doing it again. Projecting the outcome of our discussion. Perhaps John might have been there at Jane's apartment for an innocent reason. Maybe he even knew someone else in the apartment building where Jane lives other than Jane herself. Well... maybe... I thought... just, and only, maybe. What should my approach be? I had no idea.

I parked across the street from the entrance to Jane's building looking about me for signs of John. Nothing. Jane came out and crossed over to my car watching for traffic. She was her usual well-turned-out self. Neatly ironed cargo pants with actual creases. A fine shirt printed with flowers and squares in soft colors. Earrings that picked out all the colors in her outfit. Sandals, equally as elegant as mine, but also multicolored to match the earrings and the shirt.

Clothes I'd never seen before. Hummm.

Jane opened the door on the passenger side and slid into the seat.

"Hey, how you doin?" she asked.

"Just fine. Just got back from a trip to Oklahoma. Looking for relatives of JOYCE on John's behalf. Did you know about that?"

"Actually, yes, a little. I know he is trying to figure out her past. If she's being honest about who she is or was."

"So, did John tell you about this himself? Or did JOYCE or, hey how did you get wind of this?"

There was a moment of silence from the passenger seat.

Finally, in a small, still voice Jane said, "I'm not sure how much I should tell you. John came to me with a tale of sending you off to prove that JOYCE hadn't been lying to him about her past. That is what he tasked you with, wasn't it?"

"More or less," I responded. "Yes, more or less that was the assignment. Did he explain to you why he wanted to know?"

Jane said, "More or less. Mostly curiosity about who JOYCE was before he met her, that's kinda what he said to me."

"But why you, Jane?"

We had been through five traffic lights. I pulled into Caruso's parking lot, shut off the motor and pulled the key out of the ignition, as I turned to face Jane. "Why you?"

"I dunno. He called one day last week out of the blue. Said he would stop by. Said he wanted to ask me something."

"And did you find out what that something was?"

Again, there was a long period of silence. Jane glanced down at her hands which were folded quietly in her lap. She did not appear to be under any stress, answering my questions. Her voice was quiet but firm. No guilty glancing about or wringing of hands or attempts to look away.

"Look, Barb. I don't know quite how to tell you this but John... John and I... we're..."

There was a banging on my door. It made me jump.

An angry looking man in a suit and tie was standing outside my car door.

"Hey lady... are you going or coming? This is the last parking place in the lot? I need it if you don't." He shrugged his shoulders. "I don't want to be rude, but honestly are you intending to park and go in, I need to know."

I glanced at Jane and she nodded yes, so I said. "Yep, sorry to confuse you but we are going in, so I'm going to need the parking space for myself."

He shrugged one more time, turned and marched back to his car, opened the door and began with wild gestures talking to the passenger who waited inside for him. He pulled away with only a slight screech of tires.

Jane and I walked to the entrance, asked for a table, got seated and were given menus.

twenty-eight

"Would you like a drink?" I asked.

"I think I'd better," said Jane.

The waiter approached and I ordered a Lemon Drop and Jane a strawberry Margarita, and the waiter walked away.

"Want to tell me about it," I asked?

"Not really, no, no I don't," said Jane.

"Okay, then, how's the weather been lately?"

Jane smiled at my rejoinder and said "Okay, here it is."

"John came over. We talked about you and how you are getting along after the divorce. He asked a lot of questions and I tried to be truthful in my answers, trying not to quote you, but talking only about my observations. He asked if you were dating, and I mentioned Ian and how you'd met and that I didn't think it was anything serious."

"No, it is definitely unserious and also none of John's business." I looked around at the dimly lit interior or the restaurant, the ambiance flat now, no longer feeling cozy and inviting, just dark.

If Jane heard my comment, she did not acknowledge it, or react to my sarcasm. She plunged on with her story.

"Then he switched the conversation to me. How was I getting along? Was it good to spend more time with my cousin, you? Something he said made me cry and the next thing I knew he had gathered me into his arms, and we were kissing. I stopped crying and started responding to his kisses and the next thing I knew we were in the bedroom, my little virginal bedroom, and I was not acting the part of the maiden aunt, I can tell you. He had my clothes off in a second and I didn't care, and I was sorry to see him go when he left. And he calls me every day. And I am so infatuated that I don't care if he's married or even that he was married to my dearest friend-cousin, you. I am such a little slut and I don't even mind that."

Jane stopped talking. Stopped telling her story. I was glad of that. Way too much information.

I said, "Okay, we're verging on too much information. God knows I know he's charming and exceedingly competent in the seduction department."

Silence reigned until our drinks arrived. I sipped at mine. Jane took a big gulp or two of her strawberry Margarita, sat back in her seat, her color rouged and a defiant look on her face.

"Okay, friend Jane. I got no advice for you. I know the man is charming. I know he's married, but I also know from experience that is not a major impediment to him in the 'moving on' department."

"Okay, friend Barb. Let's forget about it for now. You deal with John about your thing, about the investigation, and I'll try to get my head on straight about how I feel about John. But right now, I got nothin, no way to stop caring about him, no judgement, moral or otherwise. I'm head over heels in lust or something and reason has flown the coop."

We ordered dinner and ate in silence. The food tasted like cardboard as I tried to absorb that my best and only pal was in love with my one and only ex-husband and, apparently, he shared her feelings. That seemed to put me out in the cold one more time. Ah well, what's a body to do? After we finished our meal, I paid up. We got back in the car and were half-way across town when Jane spoke up.

"Uh, I'll tell John I saw you. I'll not tell John what was said. I have to play this relationship with him by ear. You understand, don't you?"

"More than I can tell you. But keep in touch. We'll talk about whatever you feel safe talking about. And if John asks me, we met, we talked, and I don't understand any of it except we have a business relationship that I will discuss with him if he has any further assignments for me." I sounded far more reasonable than I felt. If Jane was aware of the distress I was feeling, she didn't comment on it.

We uttered neutral sounding goodbyes and I dropped Jane at her apartment. I drove on home, unwilling or unable to name what I was feeling about Jane or John or JOYCE or myself or anyone.

twenty-nine

At home I raided the house for chocolate. Chocolate is my drug of choice for bad feelings and believe me this triangle, quadrangle, whatever it was, was giving me fits. I mourned not the loss of John, long gone to me anyway, or his unfaithfulness to JOYCE... there was a wee bit of 'ha, ha your turn, bitch,' in my feeling about that situation. The loss of Jane as a friend and confidante was a whole other matter. I decided to turn to Ian. Maybe he could help me sort out my feelings. I needed to talk to someone since there was no chocolate to be found, as if chocolate was allowed to linger unmolested around my apartment for any length of time anyway. I did find one lone M and M, a green one naturally, that had sneaked into the silverware drawer, but only that one. It was not sufficient to provide any kind of cure.

I hesitated for only a minute. Surely Ian felt that I had the potential to be more than a friend. Surely I had the indicators that friendship was all I felt for Ian. Was it fair to consult him? Fair, shmair, I said to myself. Ian must take his chances like the rest of us in this battle for love and friendship and success and at least monetary parity of some kind or the other.

I called. He wasn't home. Chocolate wasn't home. Despair was about to set in.

Now came the time to make *the* bad mistake and of course I did just that. I picked up the phone and dialed John. To make matters worse, I chose at home. Of course, JOYCE picked up the phone, on the second ring. Didn't that just go with the day I was having? So, of course, I hung up.

Thirty seconds later the phone rang. An angry JOYCE sounded off. It seems I had forgotten about caller ID. My bad!

"What the hell are you doing calling here? John isn't in and God knows I have nothing to say to you. And what were you doing in Oklahoma anyway? I got a description and knew that bouncy little red-headed bitch was my husband's ex-wife from Tucson gone all the way to Oklahoma to cause a problem. Why are you bugging my brother? What is going on and what have you got to do with John? You two are through; don't you get the picture? Do I need to explain the meaning of the word *divorce* to you? I can tell you this. My brother is coming to town and he's not too happy with your snooping around at his house. You better mind your p's and q's or we'll have your ass in a sling," and with that Joyce hung up the phone. Well, slammed it down was probably a better visual, but I wasn't there to see it.

Oops, John could be mad at me, client speaks to wife of man who is paying her to investigate wife's family.

Oops, wife of man who hired me (coincidently also my ex) and subject of my investigation, has somehow figured out that I was at her brother's home poking around and is pissed off about that.

Oops, brother, and for all I know his sheriff friend, are on their way to Tucson to look me up. Hope that is 'look me up' and not 'lock me up' that he has in mind.

Oops, cousin and former bestie is going to be displeased that I stirred everything up.

Oops, oops, oops. I think I may have made a mess of things.

The phone rang again. This time it indicated that Jane was calling. I covered the damn thing with a pillow and went to bed.

thirty

Tuesday morning dawned cool and clear. A typical September day with a slight chill in the morning that would vanish well before nine a.m., but for just a moment there was a hint of fall in the air.

I hadn't slept very well. I vaguely remembered I had a date with John. Seven-thirty for breakfast. That was the plan. I don't think so. Not in the mood. Don't have a report written. Don't have a report written even in my head. Do not want to see John. Can't call and cancel. Don't want to risk having the phone answered by JOYCE, again. And was John even staying there? Too early to call Lucy. She won't be in the office this early.

And, of course, I knew that no one stands-up John ever. Not in all the years that I knew him had anyone failed to appear for an appointment. Not that he'd told me about, and John didn't have much of a filter. If someone had stood him up especially on a personal level, he would have complained loud and long to me and to whoever else would listen. So, I might be the first.

The idea of breakfast with John left me feeling panicky. Because I had sorted nothing out about my trip to Oklahoma or my relationship to cousin Jane or even what I had told JOYCE. Worse yet, I had nothing fixed firmly in my head about what she had told me. About her brother coming to Tucson to prey on me in retaliation for my visit to his house in Oklahoma. No, I had nothing truly sorted about anything at all. And John wouldn't stand for that. He would focus his handsome face in my direction, his eyes searching mine and make me tell all. And I'm not ready for that moment. Not ready at all.

So, avoidance. That's the ticket. That is my modus operandi when faced with a situation such as this. I'd have to psych myself up to see my ex. Instead my thought patterns had led me in the other direction, complete and total demoralization.

I shrugged, pulled my sweater more tightly around my shoulders and picked up the phone to call the restaurant where we were to meet requesting that word be given to John when he arrived that unfortunately Barbara Black could not be there to meet him this morning due to circumstances beyond her control. They wouldn't write all that down, they might not even tell him anything, but I had tried, hadn't I?

I was justifiably depressed. After all, my life professional, personal you name it, was out of control. I decided it was the perfect day to go to the jail and visit J. Milton Smith. How much worse could things get? That's where my logic took me. My car took me the rest of the way.

When I got there, J. Milton was willing to see me. Well, that was a plus. I filled out the form again, handed it in, used the lockers to deposit my purse and phone, gained access to the interview rooms by going through the metal detector and the long sally port, and checked in with the sergeant occupying the desk today, and then found my assigned interview room and waited.

It wasn't long before J. Milton, orange uniform and all, was delivered to my door. Frankly I was surprised he hadn't moved on to plaid, the bad boy's uniform. With his attitude I thought he might have drawn unpleasant attention to himself by now.

"Good morning," I said in the most musical voice I could muster. "How's it going?"

"What's good about it? I'm stuck in this hell hole. Bail has not been arranged though my baby-faced lawyer claims he is working on it."

His blue eyes looked directly into mine. There was no discernable warmth in them.

"I've run into a dead end. Just thought I'd check with you. I know you've had plenty of time to think. Have you come up with any ideas as to who your wife might have been meeting?"

"One. One idea."

"What's that?"

John looked down at the Formica table.

"It's about the timing. She sometimes left around six-thirty in the evening, maybe a couple of times a week. Slipped a sweater on. Put on her tennis shoes. I know 'cause she usually went barefoot around the house and only put on shoes to go outside. Claimed she felt like getting out. Felt like having a walk. She was usually only gone about an hour or an hour and a half at most, I think. I wasn't keeping track. Not paying real close attention."

He glanced up at me and then went on, his tone sounding slightly defensive.

"My writing time was afternoons and evenings. I'm not a morning person. I'd be in the study working away and she'd stop by and say things like: 'See you later.' Or 'I gotta get out of here.' or once, 'I've graded half my papers, I just need to take a walk and clear my head.' And then she'd be gone. Like I said, it happened maybe once or twice a week that last few weeks."

He paused. "On second thought, maybe for as much as a month or so. I didn't notice details like for how long or what she was wearing; her absence had no real effect on me."

J Milton looked at me expectantly, apparently desiring some kind of reaction. Praise maybe. For a recovered memory. It might just help me figure this out.

I showed him a full smile and an encouraging nod.

He sat up a little straighter.

"Evenings, like I said, my best writing time. That's when the juices are really flowing. I didn't much care. Didn't see that much of her anyway. She usually worked in the living room or the bedroom and I was in the study. I didn't pay her much mind. But maybe it means something. Wherever she was going she didn't take the car. I would have heard it leave. She walked."

"I think that might mean something. Something about the proximity of Mr. Almost Right to your house or neighborhood."

J. Milton grunted. That was his only response. He stood, walked around me and headed for the door. Not overdoing the pleasantries. He displayed good posture and still had the cutest butt in town, not an asset in prison. Maybe he was working-out here at the jail. Didn't look like he'd totally let the predicament he was in destroy him.

I felt better. I had a purpose again. A mission so to speak. And J. Milton Smith, who knew how he felt? All I knew was at least this time he hadn't given me the finger on his way out of the room. Maybe because his deputy escort was approaching, but still, it was something.

As I drove back to my apartment across the vast expanse of the city, I was grateful that I had something to think about besides the mess I was in with *JOYCE* and *John* and *Jane*.

My mind wandered and an errant thought appeared from nowhere. What is this fixation with the letter '*J*'? My life seemed about to drown in people whose names began with '*J*'. Time for a change. I swore, the next complication and or joy to enter my life that came in animal form, either human or otherwise, was going to have a name that began with one of the other twenty-five available letters.

Of course, that brought me to Ian. Time to call him back and see if he was still speaking to me. Seemed I had fobbed him off with the old "important business call I must take" nonsense. I would be lucky if I had an 'I' speaking to me.

I made it from my parking spot to the apartment with little distraction except for running into the rumored to be bra-stealing neighbor who seemed inclined to talk but accepted my friendly, "Hi... in a hurry... catch you later" phrase as I rushed past him on the landing. The light on my phone seemed to be dancing double-time when I came in the door.

I reluctantly played back the messages on my machine. Sure enough, there was a message from John. Ah yes, one of the J's and an angry one at that.

It began so lovingly "...Where the hell are you? They told me at the restaurant that you were unable to be here due to 'circumstances beyond your control'."

Of course, he went on. Not a man of few words John, my ex.

"What the hell does that mean? You had better be tied up in the trunk of someone's car or given only one phone call to make by the cop who arrested you. That's how it better be!" and the phone slammed down in my ear.

I looked for John's office number. When I called, Lucy answered.

"Oh, it's you. I thought I made it perfectly clear that this meeting was important to John. Not only will he yell at you, but he's already bitten my head off this morning. John does not like it when he is disobeyed, and I think that is how he views both of us today. Chicks who wouldn't stay in line as told to by the big fat rooster. Really sometimes he goes too far! I will put you through to him, but hold the receiver away from your ear if you value your hearing."

I wandered toward my small kitchen. The room delighted me with its neatness... neatness brought about by lack of use. Gleaming white cabinets shone brightly reflecting the light from a wide window. The counter tops were white too. They would have gleamed save for the thin layer of dust. I got a bottle of water out of my refrigerator. The better to put out the fire that was about to land all around me. It promised to burn more brightly than my hair color.

I propped the receiver between my ear and my shoulder in order to use both hands to remove the cap. Unfortunately, that left the earpiece way too close to my head.

"BARBARA," he yelled. "What on earth were you thinking. You were supposed to meet me for breakfast. I break my balls to get there on time and you chose not to show up. I've a mind to cancel our contract and not pay you a damn dime."

Now he was getting into a serious area, but I could deal with that. Lying comes easily to me when I'm under pressure.

"Look, John, I'm sorry. I got an urgent message to visit my client at the jail this a.m. You'll remember, on my other case. I tried calling down there, but I couldn't get through to my client. His life hangs in the balance. He's accused of a murder he didn't commit. So, I had to go. Too early to call your office. And your wife is downright hostile to me if I call your home, so I did the best I could and just left you a message at the restaurant. If you would just carry a cell phone like normal human beings..."

What the hell, I thought. I fell back on one of the rules that I try to live by with some degree of consistency: the best defense is a strong offense. Not exactly one of the ten commandments, but it serves me well.

I had heard sputtering in the background as I was talking. John's voice became measured and quiet. Perfectly clear diction and slow delivery of speech is a bad omen when John is involved. Time to pay careful attention.

"Okay. Here's the pitch. Either meet me in fifteen minutes and, by God, I mean exactly fifteen minutes at the same place we were to have breakfast or be prepared to pay for your Oklahoma trip yourself."

All sorts of emotional responses ran through my head as he was talking. Surely since we were no longer married, I didn't have to put up with his BS anymore. But my verbal reply was a meek "okay." No way I could pay for that trip myself. Nor should I, but still, he had the checkbook and I didn't. Can't argue with that kind of power.

Not even stopping long enough to check my lipstick I hurriedly gathered my receipts from the trip and quickly locked my door. I took the stairs rather than the elevator and dashed to my car.

thirty-one

I was a full five minutes early at the eatery of choice and began to think through what I would tell John about my Oklahoma trip. I decided quickly to censor nothing, to give him a full accounting and maybe even, whether it was called for or not, to relate my interchange yesterday evening with the less than charming JOYCE.

John entered the restaurant with a scowl darkening his otherwise handsome face. He saw me immediately. No wave of the hand, no friendly smile, he strode to the booth I was occupying and abruptly settled into his seat.

"I see you made it. Damn good of you. Now how about a report."

I started at the beginning and described my visit. My abrupt and somewhat harrowing experience of escaping the small town. My plane ride home. The adventure of the car having to be rescued by the rental agency.

As I talked, the tension seemed to slip from his face, and he began to listen in earnest. Not commenting, not nodding in approval but listening intently to my description of my experiences and the choices I had made as a result of those circumstances. I pulled from my purse the picture of the family that I had stolen from that album in the small dark living room in Oklahoma and showed it to him.

He took his time studying it.

"So, tell me again, who are these folks? Other than Joyce, of course. I recognize Joyce."

"From my research I can tell you that the brother is the younger of the two men, the one who lived in the house I visited in Oklahoma. Jackson Barnes by name. The younger woman is his and JOYCE's younger sister. The old man is, I have reason to believe, JOYCE's first or at least most recent husband before you. He is now among the missing. Supposedly he moved to Florida, but I can find no record of him there. His name was or is Jason Smith. (It dawned on me suddenly... another 'J' and another Smith, oh my god!) The younger man is Jackson Barnes, that is the brother of your wife JOYCE Barnes born Kelleman, married name possibly even probably Smith and now JOYCE Barker. So, JOYCE Kelleman-Barnes-Smith-Barker... let's see, did I miss anyone?

"Okay, I think I get that part." John Barker, in my opinion, is nothing if not quick-minded.

"Well, here are some of the bills, but I need to copy them. Lucy gave me an advance to my credit card so most of them have already been paid, in case you were still thinking of not paying me..."

John responded only with a steady, silent stare to the accusation, so I quietly dismissed that possibility.

"There is one thing more. I did call JOYCE last night. I won't make that mistake again anytime soon. I was trying to reach you. What I garnered from our conversation was that JOYCE knows I was in Oklahoma 'snooping around' at her brother's house and he is coming here hell bent on finding me and whatever might follow I don't know, but it didn't sound friendly."

John tented his fingers. After a thoughtful pause, he said, "How did she know it was you?"

"I wondered the same thing myself. From my description perhaps, the red hair. But also, in my purse I had a copy of the hotel bill, from the night before, with my current address and phone number. I left it in the car, took my wallet and went into hiding, but they must have gone back to the car and looked in my things and found it. He and that sheriff guy…"

"Well, Joyce isn't stupid. She'll figure out soon enough that I hired you to look into her background. I'll be hearing about that. I've already decided that Joyce is not the woman I want to be mother of any child of mine. This could be a very expensive divorce. So, I may use some of this background information to rid myself of Joyce. Especially if I can get her on bigamy. You see if you can find a marriage license for those two. Joyce Kelleman and that Jason Smith of near-Ardmore, Oklahoma and/or information about a divorce. And where does the Barnes fit in? Was that her name at one time?"

John answered his own question with a plausible solution.

"Maybe the Barnes brother and sister are only half-brother and sister to Joyce. Who knows? Keep looking. Keep me up to date. I have a feeling this is not going to turn out well. If Joyce's brother shows up at our house and I know about it, I will let you know. I don't know if Joyce knows where you live. Not through me she doesn't, but that information is probably in my files and I wouldn't be surprised if she had done some digging in there. Oh, and yeah, your hotel receipt. Looks like you dug your own hole on that one. But about my situation, I'll know more this evening when I get home."

John sighed. He hung his head for a moment. And then he looked up at me and there was a bit of the old twinkle back in his eyes.

"I may well be in a motel come tonight. Don't much care. Things are gonna get messy in the next couple of days."

John took a cell phone out of his pocket. "I'm texting you my number right now, so you can call me. If I can't talk, you'll know."

We had ordered lunch somewhere in the middle of the story of my adventures in Oklahoma. John's burger came and my sandwich right behind it. He took a couple of bites, laid a twenty and a ten on the table next to his plate and said,

"Take care of these for me, okay? Not much of an appetite and a lot to do. The breakfasts are really good here. You should try one sometime." He smiled at me, winked, and walked away.

I went to the counter and retrieved a to-go box, loaded it up, paid, and left a generous tip. And I too walked out of the door. Jane's name and that situation had not come up in our conversation and I, for one, was glad it had not.

thirty-two

The rest of the day passed quietly. I decided to record my adventures in Oklahoma; to document all that had occurred and what I had surmised. I feel very strongly that something may have happened to Jason Smith, something not so nice. If I had the ability to talk to local law enforcement that I could trust, I might have had them get some cadaver sniffing dogs on the scene and see if there are any bodies buried in the yard at lonesome ranch. I shuddered to think I might have ended up in that yard too. All of this was a hunch. Perhaps I had watched too many late-night horror mysteries on television in the past. Probably all a pipe dream, but something about that house, the yard and my narrow escape still sent goose bumps running up and down my spine.

Late in the afternoon, I spoke with Ian on the phone. He was a little stiff and formal. My blowing him off the other day had not left me in a positive light and my lack of responsiveness to our relationship had not further endeared me to him or helped in any way his trust level. Now was probably not a really good time to tell him I had really hit it off with his ex-wife and might enjoy seeing more of her.

Nope, I'll save that for later, or better yet, never. He didn't ask me out, nor me him. We ended our phone call with a 'see ya'. Not a promising beginning and not even a defining ending. Well, I knew how to play GWTW. I'll worry about that tomorrow.

Tonight, under last month's playbook, might have been the kind of evening that I would have taken my cousin Jane out to dinner providing I could find some coupons for 'buy one get one free.' If she had been seeing my ex, John, she was now a little out of my league, however. He knew how to wine and dine a girl and that wouldn't include any Taco Bell nights.

I went to the pantry. The cupboard was bare. I mean not even a packet of stale crackers or a three-quarters empty jar of peanut butter. Looks like I'd have to go out. Seated back on my couch again, I picked up the phone and tapped in Jane's number. I'd give her a try anyway, for old time's sake. She could and would easily say no if she wanted to.

Jane answered before Alexander Graham Bell's invention had finished its first ring.

I heard an anxious sounding, "Hello..."

"Hello," I said. "You sound agitated. What's up?"

"I haven't heard from John all day. He calls me once or twice a day and then often again in the evening hours just before I go to bed and today, nothing!"

Using my most soothing tone of voice I said,

"Well, I saw him at noon. Just to discuss the case that I was looking into for him. About mid-day. He was thinking he might have to move out of his house.

So, he could be busy doing that. And no, before you ask, your name did not come up."

"I know; I know. He and I agreed to leave you out of our love triangle. After all three's company, four's a crowd." She gave a slight chuckle at her own humor, then Jane got serious.

"I'm worried. If he was going to tell Joyce he was moving on without her, well... how should I put this? I'm worried about his safety. Joyce is not some sweet little country girl. She is mean. She's not going to lose John without a fight. He's told me to watch out for her. He suggested she might come after me..."

I tried to get a handle on this new information. "I know she's a little mean. But dangerous, did he imply she might get dangerous?"

Jane sighed. "For a PI you are a naïve sort of person. She has a gun. He says she knows how to use it. Goes to the shooting range. John hates guns. Asked her to get rid of it and she told him 'Hell no, no way, no!'

"So, what do you want me to do?"

Jane came back to me with a wail that sounded like it would reach a crescendo at any moment. "I don't know. Just do something. Find him. Find him now!"

Somehow, I got off the phone with Jane without a definite commitment to take action. What action I couldn't imagine. I'd left her with an admonition to lock her doors and not answer them and sat down again on my couch to think.

I was really getting hungry now. I thought maybe I could plan better with even a drive-in burger in my stomach, gathered my keys and headed for the door when the phone rang again.

It was Lucy, John's secretary. Aware of my lack of status in John's world, Lucy still treated me as if I had value and importance. Maybe I was grasping at straws for acceptance, but I was hoping I might begin to think of Lucy as a friend. Again, someone too close to John, but I was getting desperate for a gal friend, a confidante. Since John got all of the friends in our divorce except for my cousin, and, he'd apparently come back for her, I knew I could definitely use a friend. Listening to what Lucy had to say, however, and I forgot about *my* needs. I heard the urgency in her words.

"Listen Barbara. John is missing. He was supposed to come back to the office after he had lunch with you. We were gonna move some money around out of his joint accounts. I have access to all that stuff. That's the way he wanted it. I'm not romantically interested in John and that was all he needed. Somebody he could trust that didn't have a personal motive. Someone who could handle his money and not ever look for alimony, no disrespect meant, by the way."

"None taken, but have you tried his cell phone?"

"Yes, and with no result. It goes right to voice mail. And here's what really has me going. I checked his balance. Somebody with his debit card has removed two-hundred dollars at a time from five different ATM's around the city. He's a thousand dollars short.

Not that that hurts him much, but he'd never do that. If he needs money, cash money, he sends me or, if in a pinch he had to do it, he sure would take it all out at once from an open branch, and they were all open this afternoon. He'd go inside and get the whole thousand at once if that's what he needed. I'm thinking someone else has John's debit card."

Suddenly, I was no longer hungry.

thirty-three

"Tell you what, Lucy, I'll drive over there now. See if either of their cars are in the driveway. He thought he might be moving out tonight. Moving to a motel. I'm not sure if he meant it or was just spouting off, but I'm gonna go take a looksee at his house."

"You be careful, young lady. I don't suppose you have a gun?"

"Nope."

"Oh Barb, what's to become of you." Her sigh seemed to answer that question once and for all.

"Then watch out," Lucy added, "and check in with me on my cell. I'm going home now. I've waited here as long as I can."

I looked at the clock. Six p.m. It would soon be dark. Good, best time of day for a prowler and I intended to be just that.

I had no trouble figuring out where to go since John and JOYCE occupied what had been my house. My car might have even known how to get there on its own. Up until two years ago, I had been Mrs. John Barker though he had accomplished a lot in that short period of time. John had divorced me, acquired a new wife and now apparently was trying to lose her. A man of multiple accomplishments. Enough musing on the past. I got into my car and headed in the familiar direction.

On my way to the house now shared by John and JOYCE, I pulled into a Jack-In-the-Box line. No other cars. I settled for a bag of fries and a large coke. I figured, I had to have something to eat. Potatoes are a vegetable. And vegetables are healthy, right?

The street where I had spent many years of a happy life, was then and still is a quiet one. The house sat at the end of a cul-de-sac resulting in a triangular shaped back yard, awkward to design as an inviting oasis in the desert. Only recently had it been landscaped. I assumed the purpose was to accommodate JOYCE's elaborate entertainment plans. Most likely she can forget those.

The house is a tri-level. The front door opens-up into a vast space full of couches and other large furnishings. That room provides easy access to the kitchen and dining rooms. The master bedroom is on the top floor. Darkness shrouded the windows in the master bedroom and John's study. The living area on the street level was equally black though a faint light emanated from the kitchen area in the back of the house adding a veiled glow to the front room. A velvety blackness enveloped the basement. The dark brick exterior of the house was without light as well. Not one car in the driveway.

I drove back down the street and parked across from a house that was three houses away from John's door. I ate two more fries and then quietly exited my car still licking the salt from my fingers. Walking rapidly but quietly down the street the absolute stillness let me know that if any of my old neighbors had a dog the animal was tucked in for the night.

I walked up the driveway slowly now, carefully placing each step with tennis-shoe-quiet stealth. I had no desire to telegraph my arrival. I wanted to check the garage. Wondering if the code had been changed, I found the outside keypad and put in the old combination. The garage door slid up much more loudly than I remembered. A lamp on John's narrow workbench gleamed and shone on two cars. John's old Mercedes and JOYCE's new BMW. Nothing looked out of place, except that on the floor behind John's car there was a tarp. On the blue surface, something wet glistened in the light. I ran up to it, touched it. As I brought my finger toward my lips, I heard the door that led from the garage into the kitchen begin to open. It had always needed oiling and, in the quick moment I had to think, I was grateful that no one had gotten around to lubricating the squeaky hinge. I dashed for the garage door, quickly stepped back outside and hit the close button. Just before the door rumbled all the way back down into place, I heard the front door slam.

I heard JOYCE yell, "Who's there?" I couldn't see her, but I could picture the gun in her hand, the one 'she knew how to use.' Fortunately, I knew the neighborhood. I ran around to the side of the garage. Even more fortunately, I knew how to move rapidly in the blackness in the familiar landscape.

Sandy, the next-door neighbor, had a row of rose bushes with a slight neighborly space between bushes three and four. Even with limited light, I could see the area that had no flowers. I ran through that opening into Sandy and Bill Mitchell's yard. I could make out the shape of their picnic table as I ran past it around the side of the house and toward the gate on the front of their yard that opened into the street. I swung open the gate, relieved that someone *had* oiled those hinges. I could hear JOYCE muttering as she swung a flashlight in larger and larger arcs around the side of her house.

I heard JOYCE's melodious tones ring out in the night.

"Come out, you miserable bitch, I know you're there."

I walked swiftly down the sidewalk scurrying under one of the only streetlights in the area, glad that I had foreseen the necessity to pull my car to the curb a full football field distance from John's house. Then I broke into a run, got into my car, glad that I had not locked it thus avoiding the beep. That sound would have been loud on this silent night and brought JOYCE running toward me in a scenario I envisioned might fail dismally to keep me safe.

As I closed my car door, I heard Sandy calling out. "Is everything okay, JOYCE?"

I didn't wait to hear a reply. I turned the key in the ignition and without headlights made a u-turn and drove out of the neighborhood only turning my lights on when I reached the first intersection connecting me to a busy street.

I think JOYCE knew it was me. Think she might have heard the garage door close, probably knew the combination had never been changed since I was the lady of the manor. And the 'bitch' reference. Yeah, I think she knew it was me. But she couldn't do much about that now, other than come racing after me. Somehow, I doubted she'd do that. Still, taking no chances, I increased my speed, less worried about a ticket and more worried about the possibility of an angry, weaponized JOYCE.

I looked down at my finger. It was sticky. I tasted it thinking it would taste of oil or some kind car fluid. I'm not too well versed in those things. Power steering fluid I think is somewhat sweet. Or was that coolant? It didn't matter. The taste was distinct. I tasted blood.

thirty-four

I had to wish I knew what John's blood tasted like because I rather thought it was his and now everyone who loved John, or ever had, had to be worried about his safety or whether indeed he was still among the living.

This called for a drink. I once again surveyed, in my mind only of course, the contents of my kitchen. There was no rum. There was no coke. There might have been coffee somewhere. If a girl needed a drink, too bad, the only liquid awaiting me at home was, ugh, city water.

I decided to get a quiet rum and coke and thought of only one place I could be sure that I could have a drink undisturbed. I stopped at a Walgreens bought a pint of rum and a six pack of cokes and realized I had acquired all the means necessary to be a closet alcoholic. Hopefully I had grown out of the habit of wondering what kind of impression I was making on the clerk. Or had I? It seemed the guy at the counter leered at me as he took my money and said, "Have a pleasant evening." Was I reading sarcasm into an otherwise innocent statement?

At home I parked and entered my building. Ahead of me on the stairs was my bra-stealing neighbor. I was tempted to ask him in to have a drink with me. That speaks either to my degree of loneliness or a death wish. I knew nothing about this guy, at least nothing good though he had helped me get a chest of drawers, albeit minus the drawers, up the stairs to my apartment door and had not molested me in the process.

He went his way and I mine. I dropped the six pack on the counter and twisted off the lid of the rum. I don't know much about booze. There was a pirate on the label. Was that the good stuff? Who knew? That had always been John's department. Buying the booze and he must have bought the good stuff. That was his style. Nothing but the best for John and, at that time, for me too.

I took thirty seconds to treasure a memory and then went back to the business at hand of figuring out where John might be.

The only scenario I refused to envision was that John was already dead.

Three ice cubes, a glass, a splash of coke and a quick pour and I was back on my couch ready to think about John's dilemma. Where could he be now? If John was still in the house in whatever state, then it was doubtful that JOYCE's aggressive baby brother would have sent her out to look for me alone. Which meant that most likely the brother and John were gone from there.

Also, two cars in a three-car-garage might indicate that Jackson, JOYCE's brother, had most likely come and gone. Didn't JOYCE tell me that her brother was driving into town and would look me up. I don't know if those were her exact words or not, but I couldn't picture Okie bro on a plane. I think he would drive. Therefore, Jackson and my ex were probably on their way somewhere. If John was dead, then probably Jackson had driven somewhere to dispose of the body, and I couldn't be of any help to John.

I shook off that thought. John was alive, I told myself. Then, where else to take him, but home to near-Ardmore and the lonesome house at the bottom of the hill. The run-down place where Jackson Barnes resides. He and his mangy, mean mongrel.

It's a long drive, maybe eighteen hours. What would he do with John on the trip? Keep him in the trunk? That's irony for you. Just today John had suggested that if I didn't meet him it would be better for me if I were in someone's trunk. Now he might be in that situation. Thank God the days were getting cooler now. Maybe John could survive all the way to Oklahoma. He was in fair physical shape. I shuddered to think about whether he could be in that truck or in a rental car. Frankly I couldn't picture that old truck making it all the way to Arizona. Maybe Jackson rented a car. Maybe he...

Well that was enough speculation. I went back to the kitchen and mixed a second drink and then back to the couch to decide what it was that I could do.

My first thought was 'go there.' That's all I could do. If John was in Oklahoma, Jackson would not be expecting anyone to follow him. It wasn't necessarily the right thing to do; it was merely the only thing I could think to do.

I wondered if John could be a prisoner in his own house. But then again JOYCE probably wouldn't have come hunting me. Then she would have hunkered down in the house and remained very quiet. That's what I thought. It didn't have to be right, but it seemed to me it might be.

I set my drink down on the coffee table and called Lucy.

A groggy middle of the night voice answered my call.

"Barb, is that you? Did you find him?"

"No. But I'm guessing the brother took him back to Oklahoma so as soon as I can get a reservation for Oklahoma City I'm going."

"What on earth makes you think that he would be there?"

"Oh, Lucy. Nothing particularly brilliant. It is the only place I can think of where he might be. John is not, if I read the scene right, in his house here, though his car is. There was some blood on a tarp in the garage. There is a hugely angry JOYCE patrolling her grounds. Most likely she's also carrying her gun around ready to shoot somebody and she wouldn't mind at all if that somebody were me."

I took a deep breath garnering enough oxygen to carry on.

"So, it's an absolutely desperate move that takes me to Oklahoma. I'm running on instinct alone. I suspect they want John to sign over a lot of his money to them for the purpose of JOYCE granting him a divorce. Holding him captive and getting him to sign stuff and then turning him loose. That's the best-case scenario I can think of. After all there are so far no witnesses to his abduction if that is what it is and...." I paused and there was only silence on the other end of the connection. I had a feeling Lucy was holding her breath.

"Hell, I don't know anything. I just know I'm grasping at straws and that calling the cops in now would be a sure way to sign John's death warrant. At least my instincts tell me that as long as this is all undiscovered, John has a chance of staying alive. I'm betting on that. So, I'm going. I'll stay in touch. I've got money left from the last deposit you put in my account to get there. Might need more to get John out so if you can get the funds and send them my way, if and only if I find him alive, I'll use that money to get him back here."

"Okay. Three thousand first thing tomorrow morning on your debit card. Not enough for ransom so if you need more holler. Go for it, girl. Maybe you can find John. Getting yourself killed in the process doesn't help though, so please be careful."

I had been pacing while we talked. I sat again on the couch. "Yeah, I will. I'm the original scaredy cat. But I can't sit back and do nothing so hunch here I come."

The minute I hung up with Lucy I called the airline. Then I called Jane. She answered on the first ring. Apparently sleep had not come to her.

"John?" she said.

"No, little cousin it is I, Barbara. Listen I'm gonna be gone for a few days. But I'll be back. I've got a hint of where John is, and, you have to trust me on this, stay away from the house. Stay away from JOYCE. Stay away from anywhere where you are alone except in your apartment..."

She interrupted me. "Where, has he left to run away from me or Joyce or what?"

"Honey, if I knew that I'd know a lot more than I know now. But no, not to get away from you. That is the last thing I suspect. Just let me go do this and as soon as I know anything, I'll get back to you."

"Okay. I'll just have to trust you. God's speed. I won't hold you up with a bunch of questions when you don't know much. Could I go with you?"

I hesitated. To have a companion on this trip had a lot of appeal. But Jane, a possibly hysterical Jane if things went sour, no, probably not.

"...no Janie. You stay here. If John call's you, you let me know on my cell anything at all, any contact from John but otherwise no. I'll be in touch."

I hung up before she could ask anything more. Who's got answers. Not me

I packed lightly. I wasn't planning on spending any more time in Oklahoma than I absolutely had to in order to find John or maybe only what had happened to him. I wasn't sure how much my own safety should be a priority. I wasn't 'in love' with John anymore, but I felt some affinity for my ex and certainly for cousin Jane who was in love with him and for Lucy and for everyone whose fate was closely aligned with his. That was all for now. All the justification I could find for the risk or possibly the foolishness ahead.

thirty-five

On the way to the airport I played my mix tape of my confidence builders: *I Am Woman, Hear Me Roar,* Helen Reddy, and *I'm Still Standing,* and for good measure *I'll Walk Alone,* tunes and words that had always encouraged me in tight spots.

I tried to relax on the plane. I thought a little bit, a very little bit, about the situation J. Milton Smith found himself in and what responsibility I had for his wellbeing. Maybe I could just return his five-hundred-dollars. I'd been through the car purchase theory, the missing lover theory, the co-worker theory without finding a likely culprit. I was ready to throw in the towel. But still I had a sense of unease about that take on the situation. Maybe I owed the rude little guy some more thought, a new look at the evidence. I left my thinking there, in the land of indecision.

My thoughts went back to my ex. Realizing I would get to Oklahoma City in the wee hours before dawn this time, I was convinced of the possibility that any car rental place in the capitol city might have me on a list if they shared information with one another.

Fortunately, they don't, and this time I rented from Hertz a big, black SUV with a bench seat in the back. Would John be able to sit up if I found him in time or would he need to lie down?

I chose not to look at how preposterous an assumption I was making. That I'd find John or any clue of him, even if anyone still occupied the near-Ardmore ranch. Still, my inner self, that little voice that prompts me to move on with my life and *do something,* was nagging me to check out the last place I had seen Jackson Barnes.

After the car rental went smoothly, I found a drug store, bought a small Styrofoam cooler and several items including bandages and salves. At a hardware store I bought a knife and a pair of scissors too, to do what with I wasn't sure. I pictured the guy literally in bondage, but who knew. At the last minute I added pliers and wire-cutters. My imagination was now going wild.

At a big box store, I bought clothes and slippers that would fit John if I found him. Good thing about preparing to find my ex, I knew his sizes. At an all-night grocer I found a few more items then I put the whole assortment of goodies in the back seat, rearranging them only slightly. I drove on to a nearby McDonalds for a glass of orange juice and an egg-McMuffin. Living the high life.

The drive to the small nameless junction of two roads where the market and bar sat across the street from one another took me about two hours. Ten-thirty a.m. now, and I did my first drive by on the highway that ran right by the dilapidated house that belonged to Jackson Barnes.

There were two vehicles in the driveway, if that's a proper name for the weedy, rutted path that cars used to approach Jackson's dwelling. One was the old red truck. Parked behind it was a car that I recognized. When JOYCE first met John, she had been driving a compact car, a Dodge, somewhat rusted and looking as if it was on its last legs. I knew it well. I had followed that baby a couple of times to the rendezvous where my cheating husband met up with JOYCE. That memory made me doubt my motivation for finding John. Maybe I would kill him myself if I found him alive. I quickly banished thoughts of revenge. Later, maybe!

I went back to thinking about the car and what it meant. So probably that was the vehicle that occupied the third spot in the three-car garage and however Jackson had gotten to Tucson he had obviously driven back to Oklahoma in JOYCE's old car. Maybe creepy-kid-brother had flown into Tucson after all. It didn't really matter. He was here now. My question was, was he here alone? I was encouraged at the thought. If he had been in Tucson, and JOYCE said he was coming then he could be back here now with that very car. And John? Maybe with John in tow too.

I drove four miles past the house, and then returned. Both vehicles still sat there. I made a U-turn down the road a short distance from the house and drove by again. I drove on just to the top of a hill where I was out of sight from Jackson Barnes' house, but could still observe the goings and comings out of the driveway to the homestead.

It was there, sitting at the top of the hill that I began to wonder if the whole trip was an over-reaction to a small amount of blood. But then again, JOYCE wouldn't have been patrolling her house with a gun if John was there, and Lucy wasn't ordinarily given to histrionics and John had remained incommunicado over a period of many hours with his love interest. If there was anything I knew about John, it was that when he fancied himself in love, he was in constant attendance to the love object of the moment. In constant contact too as if giving breathing space to the adored might make her lose interest in him. Even, I reasoned, if I were on a fool's errand, I had reasons to be there. Reasons enough to be concerned, indeed even frightened for John's survival.

One other item I remembered is that for every hour I spent on finding my supposedly missing ex-husband, it was one more segment of time that I wasn't devoting to who killed J. Milton's wife.

As I pondered these things the old Dodge appeared on the road ahead of me and moved on toward town.

"Okay," I said out loud, "okay this is it." There was no one to hear me. It was time to go back to my least favorite destination and check it out. I'd come this far; only a fool would go home now. Maybe I was not so much in love with John, maybe I had put that degree of devotion behind me, but didn't twelve years of good times obligate me to find him? My answer to my own self-doubt, was, yes, of course it did.

Still, it was with fear and trepidation that I drove up that short unkempt drive. Nothing had changed from what the front of the house had looked like the last time I saw it. Weeds still had ownership in the front yard. The screen door to the porch still sagged, not totally, but like a drunk in a doorway, leaning to one side to keep from falling down.

I took my small portable cooler from the back seat without opening a door. I took the cover off, unwrapped one item so as to make it readily available. Stuck everything back in the cooler. Flung the door to the rented SUV open and quickly got out. Sure enough, the screen door slammed wide and the dog, my nemesis, was there. What had Barnes called him? It didn't really matter. I didn't have time to train my brain on remembering his name. The odious pet launched himself from the top step and with a low growl headed straight for me.

I had only to reach back inside the car, dip my hand into the cooler and retrieve the huge T-bone steak and hurl it up into the air in the dog's general direction. To my joy his forward motion ended, and he threw himself up in one smooth motion like a circus dog, and grabbed the steak in mid-air. He did give me an ugly look, it's true, as he dragged the steak off into a corner of the yard, but then he ignored me as he began to chew and tear at the steak. Raw meat was his pleasure and I was happy to provide some that did not come directly from my body.

I bypassed the dog and made for the screened porch. True, he did offer a half-hearted growl as I walked by, but, luckily, he was still tearing away at the raw meat and I was apparently just a passing fancy to him. I could almost hear him thinking. "This stuff is good. I'll get to *her* later."

I tried to pull the screened door shut behind me, but so bad was its fit that it would not come tightly closed. Opening the door to the house I saw by the dim light a sight that frightened me so much that I stood, mouth agape, at the door, as precious seconds ticked by.

There was John. Tied in a chair with his hands secured behind him. His head lolling to one side and drooping in an unmistakably corpse-like fashion. I pulled the door closed behind me and headed for the disaster that was my ex-husband.

thirty-six

As I approached John and walked around to the front of his body, he opened one eye, blinked and said, "You? Babs?"

Two good things from that. He recognized me and he gave signs of life. His voice was so muted and shaky if I hadn't been expecting it to be John, the blob in the chair would have gone unrecognized.

I took a quick survey of our situation. John sat more-or-less-upright in a chair stuck in the middle of the room. He was dressed only in his underwear, without shoes or socks. The odors emanating from his body were of sweat, urine, feces; those of an unimaginably dirty smelling derelict.

There were clothes for John which I had carried in a bag under my arm. He is a big man, but I had brought with me elastic wasted mom-jeans and an oversized shirt.

But first I took out the scissors and the knife from the cooler and making my way around the shape of John half sitting, half lying in the chair, I went to the back of that odd configuration to see how he had been secured. There was a rope around his middle. I made quick work of that with the knife. The plastic ties that secured his wrists gave way to a simple cut made by utility scissors.

As I removed the restraints John slumped head-first onto the floor. I knelt beside him, a hastily-opened bottle of water in my hand, and held it to his lips. "Drink this and then we gotta get out of here."

John swallowed a couple of gulps of the water and the rest of the liquid ran out of his mouth onto the floor. I struggled to dress him. I'm a smallish woman though I always feel I could lose a few, but still I managed to stuff Johns legs into the pants and pull them up. I didn't bother with the shirt for now. In the process of my dressing him, he ended up in as nearly a seated position as a rag doll can achieve.

"Look, John, you gotta stand up."

It had been like dealing with a long-legged rubber-doll to dress him. I pulled the chair he had been imprisoned in over towards him. I put my face down near his dirty, bearded face and said, "John we gotta get out of here. Barnes will be back and we're no match for him."

This time John opened both eyes and looked at me, again.

"Babs?"

"Yep, it's me. Lean on the chair and I'll help you stand."

He did get half-way up. I still don't know quite how because it was obvious that he was exhausted and in some other way not all there. Drugs? I couldn't tell. I didn't have time to worry about it.

With him bent nearly in two but his hand resting on my shoulder, we headed for the door. I left everything else behind except with sudden inspiration, I grabbed the second steak out of the cooler. One step onto the porch, three steps to the sagging screen door. In the shade of a near leafless tree that looked almost as bad as John, lay my nemesis the dog, nameless and still. The antihistamines, from my own supply of drugs, I had tucked into pockets of the steak seemed to have done their job. Nonetheless, I threw the second steak in his general direction and guided an increasingly heavy John towards the black SUV.

John didn't smell much better in the open air and the thought crossed my mind that I would like to vomit on the spot, but there was simply no time for such histrionics. I swallowed hard and continued our halting, awkward walk which resembled more a stumble than a method of orderly forward progress. Somehow, we got to the car. First part of the battle won.

I opened the back door, holding onto John with one hand and pushed him into the opening. He ended up draped awkwardly on the back seat. I shoved his legs in behind him and slammed the door in the same motion, hoping I wouldn't catch any part of John's anatomy in the door itself. I hiked myself into the front seat.

I had left the keys in the ignition, my purse sitting in the passenger seat. It was an all or nothing plan, but now it worked out well since I didn't have to search for anything. Thankfully, as I turned the key, the motor purred to life. Making a wide U-turn, I headed for town.

I was grateful not to see the blue Dodge on my way into town. It was however in evidence, parked, where else, but at the bar across the street from the small ancient store front. The huge Greyhound bus was parked in front of the store, small clouds of dust still puffing around each tire. I pulled the SUV as close to the door of the bus as I could get. I didn't really have a plan, just the faint hope that the same driver would be on duty and somehow could help me.

He appeared as if by magic at the door of the country store. When he walked deliberately towards the SUV, I cracked the driver's side window.

"Listen you can't park there, Lady. Now I gotta move my bus to let my passengers on." I rolled my window down all the way. He took a step away from the opening. "What is that awful smell?" And then looking more carefully at me, he said, "Not you again. What is it this time?"

thirty-seven

Like a small and needed miracle it was good ole Benny, same driver, same bus that I had used earlier. Of course, it was the same place at the same time and there was only one long-run passenger bus that came through this tiny stop in the middle of nowhere. My miracle was timing and nothing more. But it was still a magical occurrence to me, and like old friends I didn't have to explain anything to this guy. He'd already lived through my flight rather than fight scenario one time before now.

"Same dilemma," I said, "but with one further complication. Now your friend and mine Jackson Barnes has been holding this man prisoner. I gotta get him outta town, but I can double the bonus for two of us."

My bus driver friend was a man of action, not words. He opened the back door. Together we struggled to remove John from the back seat. Wordlessly, we propelled him into the bus and to the restroom, such as it was, in the back.

The bus driver grabbed a can of air freshener from the bathroom and a sign that pronounced the room "Out of Order" hung one on the door and then sprayed the contents of the can around the bus. He turned the deodorizer on himself as well.,

"The odor of your friend alone is enough to make them understand that the toilet's backed up."

Then he added, "Look, they'll be coming out of the store soon. I'll go in and tell 'em that the john is out of order and they need to use the store's facilities before they get on the bus. You take that hulking big car around to the back of the store and hide it, and then join your buddy in the bathroom before I get back. You got less than five minutes. Make 'em count."

I did exactly that. There was no one in the parking area when I got back on board the bus. But worse yet, the blue Dodge was no longer in the parking lot of the bar across the street. I locked myself in the bathroom, sat on the can and brought John's head into my lap.

John raised his head. "Whar w' goin?"

"To Ardmore, John, and then to Oklahoma City. Hang in there."

He lay his head back down on my lap and appeared to relax and possibly to go to sleep or to pass out, I'm not sure which. The fumes in that room alone were enough to cause paralysis of some kind.

I heard a knock on the door and the quiet voice of the bus driver.

"You both in there?"

"Yes," I answered in an equally subdued voice.

"Then here we go."

"Just keep your eyes open for the red truck, a beat up old blue Dodge or, God forbid, a Sheriff's squad car and if none of those appear, we should be okay."

I spoke in a voce pitched so low that the driver probably didn't hear me through the door and was most likely already walking away when I expressed my fears. But having voiced them, and with no windows or mirrors to check, I knew I had only one choice. To wait and see....

I could hear the voices of the other passengers complaining loudly of the odors emanating from the bathroom, bemoaning the fact that their pleasant trip had turned into a handkerchief over the nose situation and then, still complaining they began moving things around in overhead bins as they settled in, and soon the bus was in motion. This time there was no knock at the door, and we began our hour-long journey to Ardmore.

I kept John's head securely in my lap with one hand. I longed for a clothespin to pinch my nostrils. Since no such item was available, I pinched my nose closed with my right hand and tried mouth breathing. With my nostrils pinched closed the stench lessened to a minute degree or at least my absorption of it seemed to be reduced to an almost bearable level.

I lived in dread of the sound of a siren following us down the highway and closing in on the bus. The two-lane highway was all bumps, but there were no indications that the local law was going to interfere with our progress. The minutes ticked by slowly, moving us toward the town of Ardmore and hopeful safety. The air quality in the tiny bathroom did not improve, but I began to relax as time passed.

Someone, at one point in time, tried the door of the bathroom. I tensed praying that the lock would hold. Whoever it was went away, muttering expletives in a low voice. John did not stir at the sound of knocking or react to the fact that my body, his cushion, tensed up to a level where it felt more like a board than a bed.

We didn't stop until the bus station in Ardmore. I heard the driver encourage his passengers to leave the interior of the bus and other sounds that hinted that he was removing their luggage from the under-the-bus-bin and then someone came back inside. I could only hope that someone was Ben.

He came back down the aisle and knocked on the bathroom door. It wasn't much of a reach for me to open it.

"Look, Lady, I've got an ambulance on the way. Ardmore only has an emergency clinic and is still in the same county. I don't know who is in charge at the station. Could be that friend of Barnes. I'm not risking it. The ambulance will take you two into Oklahoma General. Let's you and I get him to the front of the bus."

Once we had brought a still limp and unresponsive John to the front, Ben handed me a slip of paper with his name and address on it.

"You can send me a check. And then I hope never to see you again. Trouble seems to follow you around."

I took the slip of paper, the ambulance arrived, and we got aboard. John was put on IV fluids and drifted off again, I was hoping his silence signified sleep and not a coma. The ambulance crew were respectful. None of the comments I had expected about the smell, but they informed me that law enforcement would have to be called when we reached Oklahoma City.

When we got to the emergency room, the attendants called the cops as they were pretty sure not much was normal about John's condition. They came; I told my story. Watching the faces around me harden in disbelief I wondered if I would end up being the accused rather than the rescuer.

thirty-eight

The detective in charge was a Walt Jefferson. I could tell he wanted to believe me but that he found my story far-fetched, and of course my principal witness was in no shape to talk to them.

After hearing me out, with some head shaking involved, and after I had given him Lucy's number and, also the Tucson Mayor's contact information he went out of the room at the hospital where we had been talking. The Mayor's contact info was one last not so idle thought I had as I was packing for this trip, knowing that the Mayor knew and respected John and would vouch for him if necessary and beaurocracy always respects beaurocracy in my experience. Jefferson left me alone at John's bedside, not even leaving a deputy with me. Maybe at least he believed that I hadn't been John's attacker.

Sergeant Jefferson returned seemingly satisfied with the results of the phone conversations he had initiated in another part of the hospital and said he would see me the next day.

John was put in a room and the rehydration process began. It wasn't until after midnight that they began to get some food into him, starting with consommé, and moving on to solids by the morning.

I placed several calls. One to Lucy, one to Jane. Jane and Lucy both volunteered, indeed almost demanded, to fly into Oklahoma City and see for themselves that John was okay. But I said 'no'. The new me that emerged from the ordeal of rescuing John was a little more take-charge than I had been in the past.

That evening Sergeant Jefferson placed a call to me to tell me that he would notify Tucson police and they would, on his say so, head out to pick up Joyce Barker for questioning. The locals had sent representatives of their own department to find Jackson Barnes and bring him in, but apparently when he had gone back home and found John missing, he had taken off for parts unknown. I asked Jefferson to inform the TPD that JOYCE was armed and dangerous, though I wouldn't have minded at all if they had to shoot her.

They were also interested in the report of a huge black SUV from a rental agency sitting behind the general store at the cross-roads near the home of Jackson Barnes, and asked if I knew anything about that. Here we go again. I hope the Mayor vouched for me too.

I caught a taxi at the door of the hospital though I noticed he rolled down all his windows when I got into his cab, He took me to the mall where I purchased clean clothes as my suitcase was still in the back of the SUV, careless of me I know, but there just wasn't time...

I bought new clothes, went into a dressing room and put them on, discarded my old ones, under-wear and all in a nearby trashcan and caught a second cab back to the hospital.

What John needed according to the attending physician was a little more rest and no histrionics. Sounded good to me. I was glad he was alive, sure that he would pay me well for my efforts, happy about how it all turned out but not at all turned-on. Several hours of sitting with the great-unwashed version of John was enough to diminish what sex appeal he had ever had for me. And that was a good thing. My infatuation, if there was any left, needed to be gone. The man was in love again, but not with me and Jane, well Jane was my dearest and only friend in the world. She could have him, and I could move on with my life maybe keeping both Jane and John in it, but not central to it.

Cleaned up or not John was not going to be my guy. He was deeply infatuated with my cousin Jane. Even though I had so enjoyed our life together I'd found when John left me that I was living a much fuller life. Even scratching out a viable existence as I was in my new role as a private investigator, I was fully employed mentally and physically and accomplishing something, meeting challenges, fully engaged in a way that I hadn't been for years. The pampered wife of a rich man was something I had left behind, and I was better off for it.

In just twenty-four hours, a cleaner, neater John was re-emerging from the shell I had brought back with me from that farmhouse in Oklahoma. I was glad to see that he was going to be all right. The doctor suggested one more day of hospitalization and he could be on his way. Once more I went out and bought clothes for John. This time slightly more fashionable ones. They would almost please him if he still cared about such details at this moment in time.

The sergeant came back to talk to him now that he was coherent. He informed John that they had sent a squad car to his house of imprisonment and found not a sign of Barnes except for the still sleepy dog. The red truck was gone and so apparently was its owner. For how long no one knew. At this point, though, there was an active seek and detain order out on Jackson Barnes.

John told them his story, how he had gone out to the garage of his house in Tucson to leave for the night, and maybe forever and the next thing he knew he woke up in the back seat of his wife's old car, trussed up like a 'stuck pig' and driven to Oklahoma. How he had been held there with only a little water and no food and felt that the water he was given might have contained drugs. That was all he remembered except he was able to give a good description of Jackson Barnes. Strangely enough Barnes had never covered John's eyes. The fact that he hadn't fed him, nor had he set up a scenario where John could not fail to identify his captor, made me wonder if they planned on letting John live to see another day.

I thought it thoroughly possible that they, Barnes and JOYCE, had not been planning on killing John but that it began to occur to them that kidnapping and murder being equal crimes, they might as well just do it.

Maybe, in the interim, she was home cleaning out their bank accounts and maybe she was contemplating a permanent disappearance for John that could not be traced back to her or to her brother. If I had found him and one of them had found me trying to rescue him, it might have been I would have been subject to permanent disappearance as well.

thirty-nine

A week after my second trip to Oklahoma City I was trauma free and settled back in Tucson. I had been handsomely rewarded by John for his rescue. Didn't have to worry about money for a while. Neither would Bennie. John had reimbursed him in a way that made it look like early retirement from driving passenger buses might be in his future.

In all honesty, I'd almost lost interest in my other John, J. Milton Smith. That case never seemed to go anywhere. Maybe J. Milton did kill his wife. I hadn't found any other likely suspect. True, lately my attention had been focused elsewhere. Saving John had taken up my time and talent. Perhaps J. Milton would forget about me just as I was willing to forget about him.

And then, I had been reconsidering the life of a PI and wondering if maybe what I really wanted to do was go back to school and set myself up as a librarian, a PE teacher, or in some other totally unrelated field.

I was curious enough about his status to find out that J. Milton Smith was out on bail. Rescued by a brother of his, a very successful dentist in another state, he was awaiting trial. He had to wear an alarm around his ankle. He had to check in daily with the Sheriff's office or the jail or some such arrangement. When, finally, I talked to him he did not furnish me with all the details.

He called me.

"Hey, Barbara Black are you still working for me? I read about your exploits in the local press but hey, remember me. I'm still hoping for some help for myself. I hired you first, remember? I'm still counting on you."

"Well, yes I do. Seems to me your parting shot the last time I saw you was to point your middle finger at me in a salute. You're still counting on me?"

"I am. I gave you a retainer, remember. Time for you to get busy and earn it."

The conversation energized me for some bizarre reason and so I merely said, "Right you are. No more lollygagging around for yours truly. I'm on it."

"Best you be. Two weeks till trial. Solve it, Barbara Black. Earn your keep."

That was enough of a direct conversation with J. Milton to hold me for a long while. I got off the phone and hunted up my notes to review what I could next do in aid of proving the innocence of J. Milton Smith in the murder of his wife Sarah Jane.

The used car or new car salesman issue seemed to have lost steam. It was too vast an undertaking and, so far, had resulted in nada but dead ends. No suspects, no evidence, nada.

There were a lot of people at the school who detested Sarah Jane, but all seemed far from the point of actually murdering her though they and some of the parents might not have been the least little bit saddened by her death. And, if this were an Agatha Christie mystery, they might have all gotten together and stabbed her once each. Surely a couple of hundred stab wounds would do in even the sturdiest of women. But, so much for that scenario, she didn't die of multiple stab wounds but of one simple well-placed bullet.

There was the photograph of the tall, but not so fat man. Her lover? Who knew? J. Milton hadn't identified him.

One other thing in my notes caught my eye. Sally Smith liked those late-night walks and wasn't going too far from home. What could that be about?

I thought about the neighborhood. I hadn't ever done a door to door survey of the neighborhood where the Smiths lived and Sarah Smith died. A Saturday morning seemed like an opportune time to wander around.

I drove to the area. Typical of suburbia, the block on which the Smith house was situated held only five houses on either side. I was in luck. On the street opposite the Smith's house every door was answered, and some member of the household appeared. Unfortunately, no one knew anything in addition to what I already knew about the night in question. I had equally good luck on the opposite side of the street where the Smith's bungalow occupied the middle position. The people to the east were home.

No one answered the door adjacent to the Smith's house to the west.

A woman wiping her hands on a dishtowel answered the door at the last house on the block.

I asked my standard questions.

"You sure waited awhile to inquire. That's been almost three weeks ago, that shooting. No, I didn't know that woman, not even to nod to. This isn't a friendly neighborhood. We all seem to go our separate ways and what with desert landscaping no one hangs out much in their front yards. And no, before you ask, I didn't hear the shot or shots that killed that woman."

I had one more question. "I've canvassed the whole neighborhood and talked to people, but the house between your house and the Smith's. Nobody's home now. Do you have any idea when I might catch someone home at that house? I mean 1511."

"Well, yeah, I do know. But you won't find anyone home there for a while. They're in Europe. Even in this neighborhood I know, because she asked me, Mrs. Johansen did, to keep an eye out for people hanging around over at her house. They're gone for about two months. She was hoping no strangers figured that out."

I thanked her. As a last ditch effort at complete coverage I dashed off a note, added my business card to it and folded the whole thing into a square forcing it in between the screen door and the front door, where maybe one of the Johansen couple might find it when they returned. As I thought that through, the note fell to the bottom and rested on the threshold. Ah well.

I drove home.

Over the weekend I gave the whole problem some more thought. I remembered that the area might be important. If Sarah Smith met someone on her walks she couldn't have gone very far.

I didn't know much about that area. Tucked behind the Smith's typical suburbia another more unusual, more affluent neighborhood existed which might best be described as country suburban. It was definitely semi-rural. In this new area, not too far away from the end of the Smith's street, were some unpaved roads. Houses along those streets were scattered out on acre or half-acre parcels. Lots of places to walk. No real places to meet up. No bars or restaurants or stores. Hmmm, I wonder.

I left my apartment, got in my car and drove.

The dog walking neighbor seemed to live near here. She had discouraged me from visiting her at home. But, I thought, that made me want all the more to do so. Call it perverse and you've got my number though my ex had called it stubbornness. Do you wonder I didn't miss him? Of course, these days he seemed to think of me as a woman of determination and persistence. Funny how his estimation of me had grown.

Mentally, as I sat in my car, I reviewed my notes on the dog walking lady becoming more and more aware that the whole picture of what had happened that night was steeped in her observations, her judgements, even her facts. She was the one who said to the police that she heard the shot before she saw the car leave with the man inside and she then described that individual in dress and person to closely resemble one J. Milton Smith or his twin brother of which he has none.

Our second encounter I'd had with the dog-walker, when I was taking pictures of the car in the carport at the Smith's home was when she had indicated she really didn't want to see me again. But I had written down our conversation as nearly as I could remember it and part of what makes me a potentially fine PI is my memory for dialogue. What had she said about cleaning up both her husband's and the dog's messes? What kind of messes? Time to look her up again... maybe a 'home visit' was in order.

I remembered that she was Lisa Manning, the dog's name was Jacque and she was married to Timothy R. Manning, professor of Agricultural Economics. Just the thought of his classes made me yawn.

The Manning's home was one of the houses on what appeared to be half-acre of lots. The dust billowed up around my car as I drove on the short, unpaved streets. What possesses a desert dweller to long for dirty, dusty streets in a sun-parched location? It's beyond me.

There was a carport visible from the street. It sat empty. No sign of any life around it, not at the moment at least. I had been looking forward to showing Lisa Manning the picture of Sarah Smith and the tall man who seemed totally enamored of one another. I had no logical reason for this. I just wanted to see the look on her face. I felt maybe she would recognize him, but for the life of me I couldn't think why. Maybe she walked the streets around here often enough to have seen the mystery man.

At any rate, it was my one really good piece of evidence about who this man in Sarah Smith's life might be. Perhaps that was who Lisa Manning had seen driving away from the sight of the shooting. I was only mildly interested in pursuing the case. But I had promised J. Milton Smith that I would try again.

I started to drive home, across town, from west to east wondering why everyone in this damn town took two cars per family and went to lunch. Well, that's the way it seems anyway.

It occurred to me on the spot, that maybe the University was a good place for me to visit. Her husband worked there. If the mystery man was from the neighborhood, Professor Manning might recognize him and save me some steps. Instead of fighting traffic on Speedway, I made a right turn onto Campbell Avenue and drove towards the campus of the U of A.

I drove onto campus, found a parking place in the library lot that did not promise to immediately tow my car away. Apparently even non-students are encouraged to read. Inside I found computers and hit the U of A catalog site. Classes listed under the name of Professor Timothy Manning met on Monday, Wednesday and Fridays for two hours at a time. God, that's a lot of boredom in and of itself but there must be people who found the subject exciting. (And I bet they were equally exciting people.) My, my, a prejudice!

I didn't have a map of the University, but I found one posted in the library and realized that the classroom or lab I sought was close by. I wondered what a lab for agricultural economics might look like anyway? What kind of specimens would be examined? Were microscopes involved? Does that suggest dollars and seeds? Who knew?

According to the map, I was, standing above the place I sought. A section of classrooms below ground level and adjacent to the main library existed. How or why it got there I didn't know. Eureka! For once the *you are here red arrow* was to my advantage. I took the short flight of steps down and entered the subterranean classroom site.

Finding room six-o-three was not too difficult. I marched myself up to the windowed door. There were tables and chairs and only one lab table with its tiny sink and what looked like a pot-filler faucet apparatus. There were a few charts on the wall, that apparently attempted to display plant diseases or diseased plants. Ugh. Neither one was attractive.

I opened the door and walked in. I'm brave, not necessarily bright, but I was hoping to pass for a student. Was I dressed dully enough for this crowd, I wondered?

Unfortunately, the professor glanced up from the small group of faces ardently hanging on his every word.

"Can I help you?" he asked.

"Wrong classroom I think," I murmured, as I glanced at the lanky man who could have just stepped out from the picture where I had seen him looking intently, might one say lovingly, into the eyes of Sarah Jane Smith.

forty

Every nerve in my body tingled as I realized who I had found. Motive, I found the motive. I know I must have glowed red. But both students and professor turned back to the work at hand. Whatever they were studying, all seemed fascinated by it. The disturbance I presented of just one more lost under-grad bothered them not at all, and I was glad to have them think of me that way. Perhaps the glow I felt was all internal, not visible at all.

Professor Manning glanced up again. A deep rumbly voice echoed across the room.

"Could I help you locate your class?"

"No... no that's all right. Sorry to disturb yours." I backed quickly towards the door, grabbed the handle and let myself out. I walked back to my car on wobbly knees. The answer had been there all along. Lisa Manning, master of lies.

So that was it really. Mrs. Manning had apparently had to clean up one too many of her husband's messes and that mess was the affair he was having with Sarah Jane Smith wife of J. Milton Smith. (Was the R. in his name for Robert, Bob? Maybe.) Mrs. Manning took the very direct route of killing her husband's mistress and when I figured that out, I decided to turn the whole kit and kaboodle over to the cops and let them do the deciding.

That became an interesting process. I have no standing with the Tucson Police Department. But I called, suggested I had some information that might help with an unsolved murder in Tucson. Gave the name of the victim and was put in touch with a detective, Lieutenant John Hoffman who I now know goes by the name of Tec. No, I don't know why, he didn't explain but as we talked, he suggested I could call him that.

I drove back downtown to Tucson Police Department headquarters across from the Community Center complex.

At first, the detective didn't see why I was involved in the matter. I explained that I had been hired by J. Milton Smith to solve the murder of his wife, Sarah Jane Smith and thereby to get him off the hook. I included the fact that he, J. Milton Smith, is presently out on bail, no thanks to me.

Then Detective Hoffman asked to see my PI license and then asked me to start from the beginning. So, I did, taking him on a journey through the trials and tribulations of trying to find out who the lover of Mrs. Smith was. How I went to her school, met the staff and found out for sure there was a lover, but not who that lover might be. How I found out about her attempt to sell her car, and buy a new one. She had met many men that way. Well she didn't seem to hang out in bars and an elementary or even a middle-school teacher didn't seem to have much exposure to eligible male partners for sexual exploits.

I told Detective Hoffman that I had met the teachers at her school and there wasn't a one I would sleep with.

That provided him with a chuckle.

I told him about interviewing the deceased's sister and how that had led to innuendo and suspicion, but no actual facts. How I had visited car dealerships posing as a woman who wanted to buy a certain make and color and age car, a Ford Focus. I was looking for a Bob as that was the only hard fact I had. That the lover or one of the lovers, if indeed there were more than one, had been a Bob.

My final clue was a picture. But before I could bring it up, Tec Hoffman called someone, and she brought him the file on Sarah Jane Smith. I could tell what it was because the name appeared written in large black Sharpie letters across the front of it. I sat silently watching as he brought himself up to date on the facts of the case. He closed the file carefully and then asked,

"So what makes you think you might have located the perfect suspect, other than the husband and from what I read he was angry, on the scene and drove away just as the body was discovered by a... a woman walking her dog I believe. A neighbor, and a person legitimately wandering the neighborhood that time of night." And Tec looked down at his watch as if wondering how long he was gonna give me to explain what I thought might be new or helpful information.

I decided to plunge on ahead hoping to keep his attention.

"Well, here's the thing," I said. I pulled my chair around closer to his desks, put my elbows on the outside edge of its large clean surface and recounted the discovery of the photo.

"J. Milton gave me the key and permission to search his house through his lawyer. He, J. Milton not the lawyer, was still in jail at the time. The house was no longer being treated as a crime scene at that point. At least there was no yellow tape up anymore. I took my cousin Jane with me. She works from time to time as my assistant though her main gig is to be a teacher's aide in a Tucson Public School's classroom. We found very little of use, except that in a manila envelope stuck in a book we found this picture. I reached into my purse took out the envelope and carefully opened the clasp. I slid the picture out of its container onto the surface of Hoffman's desk.

"The first thing I did was to take it to the jail to see if J. Milton recognized it, and he didn't claim to know the man."

Hoffman sat still as a fox watching his prey. Gazing down intently at the picture he said,

"It is rather obvious that the two of them have a fondness for one another. It's also obvious that this is not an old photo taken from an album or something. It's clean, shiny, new."

Hoffman made these observations as he stared down at the picture which he did not touch but rather had his hands placed carefully on either side of the photo. Not a man to handle evidence unnecessarily. Kinda cute too, I thought. The white line from a ring no longer worn on his left hand reminded me that the good ones are often already spoken for, but maybe someone had recently freed up this guy and he was available. The stuff dreams are made of.

"So then," I said, "I went back to my notes one more time. And it became obvious to me that the only witness to put J. Milton there at his house at the time of the shooting was Mrs. Manning, the erstwhile dog walker."

Tec Hoffman interrupted me to say,

"Since she was on the scene, we looked into her. She had a legitimate reason to be there. She has no record and has lived a respectable existence at her current address for years. She passed a paraffin test we gave her as well. She had not fired a gun in recent history. We searched the area and did not find a gun either so... we stopped looking at her."

"Well, here's the catch. I keep a record of bits of dialogue along the route of my investigations."

I said that with as much aplomb as I could pull off since the case of the murder of Mrs. Smith was my first and apparently, any good habits I had developed on this case didn't come with a long history of performing them consistently in the past. There was no past.

"One thing that Mrs. Manning said to me was that she was in the habit of 'cleaning up the messes' that both her husband and his dog were prone to make."

"And..."

I sat back in my chair, shrugged my shoulders and said,

"What's messier than an affair?"

"Mmm," Tec murmured. "What more you got?"

"Okay, the rest of this is fairly simple. I went by her house, but she wasn't home. Then I took it on myself to go down to the U of A. See if I could see the husband, maybe ask him a question or two. I did so. Found his classroom and, voila, he's the guy in the photo."

"...And, that proves?"

"Not a damn thing, but here's what I think happened. The affair is between Professor Manning and Mrs. J. Milton Smith. Mrs. Manning finds out. She decides to put an end to the affair."

"...And you think?"

"That our witness is actually our perpetrator. Now I'm a lowly PI and not prepared to prove this or set a trap to prove it. Not only am I lowly, but I'm new at this game. I figured I'd give you the benefit of my research and maybe you and your band of sleuths with your government resources can prove my hunch right or wrong."

Tec Hoffman sat there for a moment. His hands folded in front of him. Thinking through what I had told him. I decided the better part of valor was to sit in silence and wait. This guy apparently doesn't jump into action. There was no attempt to call for and grab a squad car, sirens screeching, lights blazing and go make an arrest... nope, not this guy"

He looked up. Again, I noticed the sandy brown, hair, the sturdy broad-shouldered build, the even features and freshly shaved wholesome look of him and felt a moment of *hey,hey,hey.*

"Do you think the Professor had any idea who you were or would say anything to his wife about your visit to his classroom?"

"Not unless she has mentioned me to him. There was that time when I was wiping down the victim's car to get some dust off to take a picture of it and I had my blouse off and was standing there in my bra and she came along."

Tec's handsome eyebrows rose, and a quizzical expression appeared on his face.

"Okay, that's one incident I didn't share with you and I will if you like, but if they were in the habit of sharing anecdotes from their day and I was a funny one to her and she was good at descriptions... well maybe then. But that's a lot of maybes and I think probably not."

"That's a story I'd be interested in, but... another time."

I had the presence of mind to blush, as his eyes met mine.

"It's just possible that while we did take a look at her, it wasn't a close enough look. Maybe she wore gloves so there was no residue on her. Maybe she washed up somewhere. She's the one who called us. She called us within very close proximity of the time of the shooting. But there could have been five or ten minutes in there and we wouldn't know. If she had a pre-plan of where to put the gun and gloves, she could have done that and still appeared breathless and excited when she made the call.

"And maybe we exhibited a little tunnel vision there. It so often is the husband or wife. And here the husband had just left after an argument with his wife and the dog walker said….

"Well, here's what I'm going do. I'll follow up on what you've told me, and I'll get back to you with what happens next."

Tec rose from his desk, reached across it and shook my hand. Believe me physical contact with him was desirable, but he didn't linger over the handshake or raise my hand to his lips…, and, well, what can I say? I'm a rapid fantasizer. I walked out of his office feeling like my duties might be done. Yet I was still hoping I would see the handsome cop again.

I left Tec to review the evidence. Lisa Manning had successfully pinned the killing on J. Milton by describing his proximity to the shooting and the timing of his departure. Easy for her to say as she was lying like a leaking sieve and no one caught on. The cops thought she was the reliable witness when actually, she was the perpetrator. I still wonder how she got rid of the gun, and assumedly gloves, in the time it took her to report the crime to the cops and await their arrival at the scene. Clever girl. My bet is she knew the area well and had picked out a spot where that very night she could retrieve the evidence and hide it at home to dispose of later. At this point no weapon has been located.

The following week, when I returned to Hoffman's office a Sergeant Alvarez left me while he went to find Tec. I walked around to the other side of his desk and glimpsed a photo of a very attractive tall and slender red-head, and another of a smallish boy, maybe ten or eleven years old. So much for fantasy.

After a week of pondering, researching, whatever cops do, they decided to arrest Lisa Manning for felony homicide and release my client from his obligation to the law. I didn't get all the details, but that's cops for you. Maybe it would all come out in the trial.

I phoned the young attorney.

"What's zup," he said.

So much for preliminaries.

I said, "You should be hearing soon from a Lieutenant John Hoffman of the Tucson Police Department. They'll be dropping the charges against your client. They've got a newer and more promising suspect, thanks to yours truly. When you inform J. Milton Smith that he's going to be a free man, you can tell him he owes me. I will be sending him an itemized statement to his home address. Thanks to me, he now can permanently have an address that does not involve his being in prison or in jail."

I'm back to seeing Ian. He's forgiven me for being distracted. He's *my* tall lanky lover now and we're quite content to see one another on weekends. He understands that my calling in life is a wee bit dangerous, and terribly all-consuming at times and I'm not willing to give it up. He's a little dull, well more quiet than dull, a little proper but steady and caring. Neither of us wants marriage again. We just want friends with privileges. I had to give up on becoming a friend with his ex-wife. Though I did like her too. It just seemed somewhat inappropriate.

Ian has convinced me that ownership of a gun might be an excellent idea. And, of course, knowing how to use it would be exceedingly useful as well. I'm still on the fence with this one. Naturally I have to admit he is quite right; but something in me doesn't want to go armed with anything but my wits and good intentions. You know where that will get me.

JOYCE's brother is still missing out there somewhere. John got an annulment or a divorce or whatever. (Grounds having something to do with the fact that his bride was complicit, even helpful, in allowing him to be kidnapped and quite possibly arranging for him to end up as dead as the proverbial doornail). The cadaver dogs did have a go at the grounds of the pathetic little ranch near Ardmore. They found nothing. Wherever Jason Smith is, he is not buried on his old farm.

John and Jane quickly got married. There's a new Mrs. Barker now. The third one! They are expecting that baby he decided he wanted, and I've no doubt Jane does too. They'll probably name her Jessica. One more J in the story.

I'm still friends with Jane. But it is her new life that absorbs her. She quit her job. Looks excellent in maternity clothes, still pressed and polished. I know she tries not to drool over John and her life with him when I'm around. But she wants to. She probably needs a new friend or two who can see all of this dispassionately. As satisfied as I am with my new life, its new direction, my relationship with Ian, there are still some mixed feelings when I see Jane in the role I once occupied. If human emotions were easy to control or just simply one way all the time... but they're not. I don't want to be Mrs. John Barker anymore, but still I cannot totally distance myself from the old me and what I wanted then. It's complex and confusing and puts a little bit of a wall between Jane and me. And that is just simply how it is.

In reference to my first ever homicide case, Lisa Manning is under indictment for the murder of Sarah Smith. And she did it too, by God; but can it be proved beyond a shadow of a doubt? No weapon found, no eyewitness. By no means an open and shut case. And a jury, they might have pity on her. The wife of a cheater. I have pity for her and even a little envy. Still I'm glad I never got around to killing John. I'd have gotten caught; they so often do. And I'm sure Jane and that soon to be born baby girl are glad I didn't carry my anger that far.

Oh, and J. Milton is still hedging about paying my bill. Guess he's free now and has forgotten the details of our arrangement. I still send him a bill once a month for saving his worthless little, but oh so perfectly shaped butt. But so far one additional payment of two hundred dollars and then nothing. The good news is he never got to see me naked or me him either, thank heavens.

I've got an office now. Downtown on Congress Street. Right in the heart of the action. No new accounts yet but I got a feeling that saving John and then solving my first case for J. Milton Smith, getting him out of jail and jeopardy, will lead soon to bigger and better things.

forty-one

A few weeks slipped by. Sitting on my couch one day, hoping for new business I couldn't help but reflect on the status of the Sally Smith case. I knew we had left a few of the important details incomplete but I could only frame the questions. I had no answers.

For instance, where did the gloves and the gun go? There had been no satisfactory answer for a long time. That was a question about to be asked at trial by the defense team who were probably considering themselves to be in the cat-bird seat with that one question as still unanswered. A lack of proof they were sure to point out. Sure, a body and a phone call reporting the body and there appeared to be a relationship between the defendant's husband and the deceased. But no smoking gun. No gun at all, and the relationship alone was not enough to snuggly tie the criminal act to Lisa Manning.

It was about three weeks after the arrest of Lisa Manning that a Carrie Johansen called me.

"Barbara Black, Private Investigator, may I be of service?"

"Ms. Black? I found your business card and a note in my door. And then I found something else that might interest you and the police, but I decided to call you first." She went on...

"My husband and I have just returned from our life-long dream of a cruise around the world to celebrate our fiftieth wedding anniversary.

"I came back to find in catching up with the news, that Lisa Manning had been arrested for the murder of my next-door neighbor. Which explains why my house plants are as dead as my neighbor woman. A few days after we got home, I found a cloth bag, burlap to be exact, under my sink in the kitchen, and inside it a gun and a pair of leather work gloves in a small size, too small for my hands anyway."

I interrupted.

"And, this is a gun you had never seen before?"

"Yes, that's right. And the key to my front door is missing and so is my house-sitter, who coincidentally sits in jail awaiting trial. Her name is Lisa Manning.

Now Carrie Johansen had my full attention.

"Mrs. Manning was house sitting for you?"

"It's a longish story..."

"Mrs. Johansen, I'm all ears. I have plenty of time to listen. Tell it however you want to."

"Well," she said, "I was never a fan of Lisa Manning, a solemn, ungracious sort but I ran into her repeatedly at faculty parties and found out in general conversation that she lived in our neighborhood and often walked her dog right by my yard. I asked her if she would mind house-sitting for me for a period of about two months while we were away. But not much to do really. Just to come in, even with her dog in tow and water my house plants. I promised to gather all the plants in my house and leave them on the kitchen counter. The task would involve her for maybe five minutes, two or three times a week. She agreed after I offered her a small recompense. End of story I assumed. But now I think there may be one more chapter and you might well be interested in it."

"Have you just peeked into the bag, or have you pulled out the gun and examined it? I'm thinking about fingerprints."

"Oh, dear, I *have* handled it. And the gloves too. Even tried one on to see if they were some of mine. They're bulky like gardening gloves and they don't fit me at all. And, of course, the gun is not mine. I don't even own a gun."

"Well, I must say, your story does intrigue me. If I could come and visit you. Which side of the Milton Smith house is yours on... though come to think of it... you're in the house on the west side of the bungalow, right?"

"That's correct."

For a moment I sat in silence. Then I offered to come see her right away.

"I think it might be best if I come over and we drive down to police headquarters and have you relay your story and give the physical evidence to a Lieutenant Hoffman, who's in charge of this case. I'll call him and tell him we're on our way. He'll probably want to interview you, but I can stay with you in case you're at all uncomfortable with the situation."

"Fine, I'll be here. But I'm not worried. At the time of that unfortunate incident I was in Greece and the stamps in my passport will prove it. I don't think I'm at any risk of being accused of the crime."

"I'll be there shortly."

I hung up and then called Tec and got right through. He informed me that he would be waiting at his office for Mrs. Johansen. Meanwhile, he promised that he would call and find out if Lisa Manning was still in jail.

"I think it's possible that she just got bonded out. I'll call and check. If she is on the street, she could present a threat to Mrs. Johansen. You be careful in that neighborhood." He paused. "On second thought I'll meet you there in say forty, fifty minutes at the most or perhaps you shouldn't even go."

I gave lip service to his suggestion. "Okay, I'll stay here" and I hung up. Thought about the situation for all of a full minute and decided I wanted to be there. I'm not a risk junkie, but Carrie Johansen had put her trust in me, and I had told her I was coming.

I literally flew down the stairs of my apartment building, almost knocking over the bra-thief-or-possible-innocent-of-that-crime person who for some stupid reason was standing unmoving in the middle of the stairs. I rushed to my car and headed quickly to the J. Milton Smith neighborhood. As I turned the corner I glanced at the driveway of the Smith's house and saw his van parked there. Maybe I should threaten to repossess it to get my back pay.

I pulled into the driveway of the Johansen house and noticed a car parked there. The driver's side door was open as if it had been abandoned in a hurry. I immediately forgot about J. Milton. I approached the house, saw the front door wide open and walked inside calling Carrie Johansen's name.

I stepped through the archway into the quiet of the living room only to find Lisa Manning standing there holding a gun and pointing it in the direction of Carrie Johansen. She looked at me, an odd little smile tugging at the corners of her mouth.

"You? Meddling again? Take a seat next to that one." She gestured with her gun at the empty seat on the couch next to Mrs. Johansen.

I hesitated, then paused to take in the scene.

"Move your ass! Sit on it too!" Again, she pointed to the couch using the gun to show me the way. "Yeah, right there on the couch with your new friend."

I moved. I sat next to a tall blond woman who I assumed to be Carrie Johansen. She was dressed in a housecoat and slippers. Given her apparel, I figured we were in her house. My genius at work again. She didn't look frightened. She glanced sideways at me and then resumed a calm stare in the direction of Lisa Manning.

"Pardon my appearance," Mrs. Johansen said in an aside to me, with her eyes still focused on Manning. "I was just out of the shower and preparing for our drive downtown..."

Lisa Manning interrupted, "You ain't going nowhere. Neither of you."

She squared up her stance. Pointed the gun at Carrie Johansen then again at me. "I don't know which of you to honor with the first shot. But you," and she gestured at me with the gun, "You annoy me the most; let's let you go first."

I only had a few seconds to gather myself together. To do what? I wasn't sure. Throw myself at her. Attempt to grab the gun. Or to get between Carrie Johansen and the gun. Any of this would have been difficult if not impossible from a sitting position. As I weighed my options, I saw her cock the gun and then the gun clicked on the empty chamber. A click, then another one...

"What the hell," Lisa Manning uttered. She began shaking the gun as if that would make it fire. And again, click... click.

Carrie Johansen rose, crossed the room and calmly took the weapon from Manning. She turned to me. I sat on the couch still shaking, aware of how close I had come to dying.

"I said I didn't own a gun. Not now. But I have owned several in the past. And, so, when I first found it, I took the shells out. Loaded guns are dangerous to leave lying around, wouldn't you agree?"

Her eyes twinkled as she stepped back from Lisa Manning with the gun now held down at her side. "When I went to take my shower to go with you downtown, I foolishly left the bag and its contents on the coffee table here," and she gestured to the table that would serve to separate those on the couch from where Lisa Manning was standing.

"This one didn't knock, but apparently just walked on in from the street, saw the bag, and took the gun out and when I came into the living room, she was standing there pointing it at me. I knew it wasn't loaded so I let her present her little play. When you arrived, you didn't knock either. I had no way to tell you..."

The doorbell rang and interrupted her.

Tec and his companion, who he later introduced as Bill Jenkins, were standing outside the door. I invited them in. Lisa Manning tried to scurry on by them. Bill Jenkins reached out a hand to detain her. She blustered a bit, shook her arm in a vain attempt to dislodge his grip, and then settled down.

The story got sorted out and the burlap bag, the gun, the ammo for it brought into the room in a plastic baggie where Carrie Johansen had stored it, were all turned over to the team of policemen. Jenkins and Hoffman left, taking the evidence and Mrs. Manning with them. They were going to stop by the jail and book Mrs. Manning again so she could take up residence in familiar lodgings. Hell, her orange jumpsuit was probably still warm.

Carrie and I, on a first name basis now, agreed to meet the detectives at headquarters.

On the way down to police headquarters she said,

"I think I made the problem worse for Mrs. Manning. We weren't expected home for another two weeks, but when we got to New York and faced the fact that we had planned more weeks of travel in this country to visit family and friends... it was just too much.

"My husband, Gary said, 'No way. I want to go home now. Enough already.'

"I had to agree. So, we came home. I rather imagine Lisa Manning was thinking she had a little more time to retrieve the gun and get rid of it permanently. And a few more days and she probably would have done just that. Boy, am I glad I made contact with you. By myself I might not have been able to fight her off, and I rather imagine she wouldn't have just stood there when the gun failed to shoot me. We'll never know, will we?"

That last question was certainly rhetorical, so I didn't bother to answer it

We spent close to six hours at headquarters. On the way home we were silent. At her door, I gave her a hug. Probably not out of the PI handbook. But I was glad we were both alive. If it hadn't been for her foresight to remove the ammo from the gun, I'm not sure either one of us would have been here. We might well have found ourselves cemetery bound.

Tec Hoffman filled in the rest of the details later in a phone call.

After Carrie and I left his office, he then called the City Attorney to tell him that the presumed murder weapon had been found. Forensic tests would verify that information. Remaining bullets replaced in the gun were test fired. The resulting lands and grooves matched to perfection the bullet removed from the body of Sarah Jane Smith.

This bit of information was disclosed first to the city's attorney and then to defense attorneys, thus their main defense claim was destroyed. When Lisa Manning's prints were found on the gun itself the impressions were somewhat smudged by those of Mrs. Johansen, who had fortunately been several continents away at the time of the murder and could not by any stretch of the imagination be considered a suspect, but there were enough partials to match up to those of Manning. To further incriminate her, traces of skin cells matching her DNA profile were found inside one of the gloves. That was icing on the cake.

Tec Hoffman shared these details with me. I don't know if he had to do so or just opted to, but I'm grateful he did. It would seem he was equally grateful that I'd handed him the actual perpetrator of the crime on a platter and it still amazes me that not only the police, but I too, took Lisa Manning at her word. It could be that J. Milton Smith is not a hell of a lot more likeable than his deceased wife, making it fairly easy for the police to believe he must have killed her. And if he doesn't pay me soon, I may begin to regret that I had a hand in clearing his name.

Jackson Barnes on the other hand has not been located. And the FBI is involved now. Kidnapping across state lines brought them in. But Jackson's sister, JOYCE, my nemesis, sits in the Pima County jail awaiting trial on assault, conspiracy to kidnap and a few more charges as a result of her treatment of my ex-husband, John. That mental picture of her sitting there, dressed all in orange is so pleasing to me. On a daily basis, it warms the cockles of my heart.

about the author

Born in Washington, D.C. and reared in McLean, Virginia, Bonnie has written with enjoyment and gusto through two colleges and three careers but now devotes herself to the written word full time. She lives with her husband of nearly 60 years in Tucson, Arizona.

She is the author of five novels. The central character is a fictional detective working for the Tucson Police Department as the lead homicide detective. This book is the first in a new series. It's heroine, Barb Black, is just beginning her career as a private investigator.

More Books by Bonnie Edwards

~ Deadly Duo Series ~

Deadly Payback

Deadly Pairs

Deadly Patterns

Deadly Playmates

Deadly Paths

Made in United States
Orlando, FL
30 July 2023